By Kimberla Lawson Roby

KIMBERLA
LAWSON
ROBY

Too Much of a Good Thing

HARPER

An Imprint of HarperCollinsPublishers

This is a work of fiction. Names, characters, places, and incidents are products of the author's imagination or are used fictitiously and are not to be construed as real. Any resemblance to actual events, locales, organizations, or persons, living or dead, is entirely coincidental.

HARPER

An Imprint of HarperCollins*Publishers*
10 East 53rd Street
New York, New York 10022-5299

Copyright © 2004 by Kimberla Lawson Roby
ISBN 978-0-06-226846-4

First Harper special mass market printing: February 2013
First Avon Books paperback printing: February 2005
First William Morrow hardcover printing: January 2004

Printed in the United States of America

Visit Harper paperbacks on the World Wide Web at
www.harpercollins.com

10 9 8 7 6 5 4 3 2 1

For my husband, Will
Life would not be the same without you.

Too Much of a Good Thing

Prologue

Curtis raised the volume on his big-screen TV, slouched farther into the sofa, and sighed with much frustration. He hadn't slept peacefully in weeks. But he knew it was all because he'd been tossing and turning, night after night, trying desperately to dismiss the voice he kept hearing. It was a voice that demanded his return to the ministry.

For four long years he'd been trying to appreciate the fifty-thousand-dollar salary he earned as director of a delinquent teens facility, but it just wasn't working. It wasn't working because during his pastoral reign at Faith Missionary Baptist Church, he'd become completely accustomed to earning three times more than that—not to mention the thousands of dollars he received in love offerings. He could still remember how most of the members had worshipped the ground he walked on and how loads of women in the church had openly thrown themselves at his mercy. He'd tried to fight them off as best he could, but it wasn't long before he'd given in to Adrienne Jackson, the wife of one of the deacons. Then there was Charlotte, who was all of seventeen when he'd first begun seeing her and only eighteen when she gave birth to his illegitimate son. But he regretted nothing the way he regretted being caught on videotape having sex with two women he didn't know. He'd met them at a convenience store and taken them straight to a hotel, but what he hadn't counted on was their setting him up to be blackmailed. Monique, his disgruntled church secretary, had masterminded the entire scheme, and Curtis had lost everything: his tax-free six-figure income, three-thousand-plus congregation, custom-built dream house, and, most important, his wife and daughter to another man.

Curtis cringed at his latest thought, and then returned his attention to BET's morning inspiration segment. A world-renowned TV evangelist danced across the pulpit. Curtis had watched four others do the same thing every hour on the hour, and wished he could trade places with any one of them. He watched one massive audience after another rising to their feet, clapping, screaming, and giving high praises to God and the minister who was speaking before them. He watched so intensely that he was now drunk from all the excitement. These people on television reminded him of his own flock, the one he used to have, and he missed having them praise him in the same fashion. He missed the emotional high he always felt whenever he stood before his loyal congregation.

He continued watching the program and envied the evangelist, who wore the same type of suit he'd once worn himself. It had been a long while since he was able to buy anything that cost a thousand dollars, but that was finally about to change. He'd recently been approached by the deacon board of Truth Missionary Baptist Church. Truth was a church that had been founded by approximately one thousand of his former members, right after he was ousted. They were members who either hadn't believed the rumors they'd heard about him or who merely felt that he deserved to be forgiven the same as anyone else. They'd approached him about being their leader back then, too, but he'd declined when he decided that he no longer wanted to preach. Now, though, their charter pastor had left and taken a position at a church in D.C., and they needed to replace him.

For two weeks Curtis had debated whether he should accept their more than appealing offer, but in all honesty, he really didn't know how he could pass on it. They were offering him five thousand per week, his choice of any luxury vehicle, and a very respectable housing allowance—something he hadn't been able to negotiate at his previous church because they'd wanted him to live in some modest church parsonage. They were even willing to overlook the fact that he wasn't married as long as he found a wife within the first two years of his contract. But Curtis didn't see a reason to wait that long and was sure that Mariah Johnson, the woman he'd been seeing for the past six months, would jump at the chance to marry him. As a matter of fact, she'd be perfect, because, unlike his ex-wife, Tanya, she knew her place. She was meek, mild, a bit naïve, and completely submissive. She was beautiful but didn't know it, and the fact that she honored God and always tried to do the right thing wasn't going to hurt.

Curtis thought about all the rewards he was going to reap and wondered why he was still somewhat hesitant. But deep down he knew what it was. It was his mother and the scripture she had quoted him over and over, whenever he spoke about his desire to be filthy rich. She quoted Mark 8:36: "For what shall it profit a man, if he shall gain the whole world, and lose his own soul?"

But the more Curtis thought about it, the more he realized that Mark 8:36 really didn't apply to him. It didn't apply because he had no desire to gain the whole world.

He only wanted a very small part of it.

The part that rightfully belonged to him.

Chapter 1

Mariah Johnson Black smiled proudly as her husband neared the end of his morning message. It just didn't seem real, him actually being senior pastor of Truth Missionary Baptist Church or that he'd chosen her to be his wife. It didn't seem real that he'd wanted a woman who'd grown up in a run-down two-bedroom apartment on the West Side of Chicago that also housed her single mother and five siblings. But he always reminded her that he'd grown up with nothing himself. Still, every now and then, she had to pinch herself, because she couldn't believe how happy she was. She couldn't believe they'd only been married six short months, and yet Curtis had already bought her a six-thousand-square-foot house in Covington Park, the most expensive Mercedes that Daimler manufactured, and best of all, she didn't have to work for anyone. All she had to do was be the best wife she could be to Curtis and the best first lady to their congregation—two things Curtis said his first wife, Tanya, wasn't capable of. Mariah almost felt sorry for Tanya, because she couldn't imagine how painful it must have been, once Tanya realized what she'd given up. Curtis had told Mariah about Tanya's affair with James, and Mariah couldn't understand how Tanya even considered being with another man. Especially when she had someone as fine-looking and considerate as Curtis. Especially since he had only been with another woman—Adrienne—on two separate occasions. Curtis had told Mariah how he'd apologized and tried to explain everything to Tanya, but that she wasn't willing to forgive him. He'd tried to make Tanya see that this random act of adultery had only occurred because Satan was trying to attack him and their marriage. He'd told Tanya that the only reason God had allowed it to happen was because He wanted to see how strong their faith was and how committed they were to each other as husband and wife.

But thankfully, all of that was behind them now, and while she wasn't happy about Curtis and Tanya's marriage ending in divorce, she knew it was the only reason she was now sitting on the second pew, dressed in a royal blue suit, a matching hat, matching purse, and matching three-inch heels. Mariah also knew that Curtis would never have paid her the least bit of attention if they hadn't worked for the same agency. He'd told her more than once that she was beautiful, but she knew it was only because he felt obligated to do so and not because it was true. She'd been a bit on the heavy side growing up, and her schoolmates had teased her daily. So by the time she was a teenager, she'd lost all confidence in herself and in the way she looked.

But in terms of her feelings for Curtis, she'd actually liked him from the very beginning and had fallen in love with him right after their first date. He was strong, compassionate, tall, dark, and handsome, and from that point she started praying for their relationship to become serious. She prayed that God would give her Curtis even if it meant she had to go without something else in life, whatever that had to be. So when he asked her to marry him, she knew for sure that God answered all prayers.

Mariah watched Curtis twirl his hands, demonstrating what he was saying.

"God will allow you to experience every twist and turn in the road until you are as strong as He needs you to be . . . until you are strong enough to deal with any trial or tribulation thrown your way," Curtis said. "And when it comes to success and prosperity, we have to take the same attitude. Sometimes we find ourselves climbing higher and higher in our chosen careers and all of a sudden a monkey wrench is thrown into the program. And of course, we as human beings don't understand it. We don't understand why God would give us such great success and then, for whatever reason, take us down a notch or two. But the best way I can explain it is to tell you what I heard on the radio last week. I was driving along, listening to 106.3, and it was then that I heard T. D. Jakes make one of the most profound statements. He said, 'A *setback* is a *setup* for a *comeback*.' "

The congregation roared with amens and a good number of people waved their bulletins at Curtis, agreeing with what he was saying.

Curtis thrived on member participation and repeated in song what the crowd wanted to hear him say again. "I *said*, a *setback* is a *setup* for a *comeback*."

"Oh, thank you, Jesus!" one woman stood and yelled out.

"Glory be to God!" another added with her hands lifted toward the ceiling.

"Boy, you know you workin' that Word on us today!" an older gentleman offered.

The organist played a few notes, and Mariah stood with her hands on both hips, waving her head from side to side with quick movements, giving Curtis approval. Then a woman jumped from her seat, shouting her way across three people sitting on the same row. This, of course, was all Curtis needed to see in order to switch into his deep southern preaching mode. He'd told Mariah that he thought it was totally ridiculous to sing the ending of every sermon, but that he'd learned during his days at Faith that his older members didn't feel like a pastor could preach if he didn't do a little whooping and singing with it. And since his older members were the major tithe and offering contributors, he gave them what they wanted.

"I saiddd, that Godd, will allow a setback, which is a setup for a great comeback. I heardd the Bible say, we may endure for a night, but joyyy, I saiddd, joyyy, will come in the morning," Curtis sang, and then broke out of the pulpit, sobbing and running around the full length of the church, hugging himself tightly. Mariah did the holy dance back and forth across the front of the church, and ten other people did the same thing up and down the center aisle. The spirit was moving frantically throughout the entire church, and continued for almost twenty minutes. Finally, everyone began settling down, and Curtis stood up from where he'd been kneeling and walked back into the pulpit.

"Oh, I tell you, the Holy Spirit is in here today, church," he announced while wiping sweat from his forehead and neck with a white Ralph Lauren bath towel. One of the women in the health unit had brought it over to him, and Mariah was glad they'd remembered to purchase a stack of them. Curtis had mentioned that the generic ones they'd been bringing him each Sunday were much too rough, and that he would much rather have something made by one of the top designers. That way, he wouldn't have to worry about the quality after they'd been washed a few times.

"There is nothing like a visit from the Lord," Curtis continued. "There is nothing in this world that can compare to being in His presence."

"Amen," the congregation spoke in agreement.

Mariah was filled with so much joy that she wanted to burst wide open. She was sure that life could never be better than it was today.

Immediately after church, Curtis and Mariah had gone over to Deacon Taylor's house to have dinner with him and his family. Deacon Taylor was one of the deacons Curtis had appointed just before he lost his position at Faith. The deacon was very loyal to Curtis and dedicated to the church, and he was the primary reason Curtis was now pastor at Truth. He, along with hundreds of Curtis's former members, had requested that Curtis be considered for the job.

Curtis and Mariah had spent three hours visiting with them and were now walking through the kitchen doorway of their own home. Usually they had afternoon or evening services to attend on Sundays, and Mariah was thankful that this was one of those rare instances when they didn't.

"Come here, you," Curtis said, grabbing Mariah playfully yet passionately.

Mariah always felt like melting whenever he pulled her into his arms. She felt so loved and so secure.

"Have I told you how much I love you?" she asked, gazing at him.

"No. Not today, anyway," he said, smiling.

"Well, I do, Curtis. I love you from the bottom of my soul, and all I want is to make you happy."

"Baby, you do make me happy. You've done that since the first day we started seeing each other."

"I really hope so, because I've heard so many women talking about how easy it is for a man to become bored with his wife. And I don't ever want you to feel that way. I want you to tell me if there is something wrong or if there is something I can do differently."

"Look, Mariah, I love you just the way you are. Believe me, I have no complaints."

Mariah sighed with relief.

Curtis removed her blazer and pecked her on the lips. Then he kissed her neck and her chest. Mariah moaned with every show of affection. Curtis unbuttoned her silk blouse, reached under it, and unsnapped her bra. He caressed her breasts roughly, kissing her at the same time.

"Do you want it here or upstairs?" he teased.

"Upstairs," she answered.

"No, I think we'd better take care of each other right here. Don't you?"

"No, sweetheart. Let's just go upstairs so we can be more comfortable," she said, pulling him close and kissing him.

"Okay, but first let me watch you undress the rest of the way."

Mariah always felt fat and uneasy whenever Curtis asked her to do this, but she went ahead and slipped off her blouse, bra, and skirt. Then she removed her nylon hose and panties and took a step toward him.

"No. Don't move. Just let me look at you. Let me look at what God created," he said, relaxing on the sofa and locking his hands behind his head.

"Curtis," she pleaded.

"What? Can I help it if I want to see all of you from head to toe? Because you really are beautiful. Your body is perfect."

"You know this embarrasses me," she told him. Not to mention she didn't think stripping like some nightclub dancer was something a pastor's wife should be doing, anyway.

"But why does it embarrass you?"

"Because it does."

"Well, you might as well get used to it, baby, because the main reason God created Eve was so she could pleasure Adam. So, satisfying your husband is part of your duty."

"I thought Eve was created so that Adam wouldn't be lonely, and so he would have a companion?" Mariah asked.

"Companionship, pleasure. Call it whatever you want, but it all means basically the same thing."

"I guess," she said, losing the mood because of all this conversation and because he was staring at her.

"Come here," he said, reaching his hand out to her. "I hate to say this, but I wasn't truthful with you earlier."

"You weren't truthful about what?" she asked, and sat down next to him. She felt nervous and wondered what he was referring to.

"I wasn't being truthful when I said that I love you just the way you are, and that I have no complaints."

Mariah was speechless, because the last thing she wanted was for him to be dissatisfied with her.

"You still haven't given me oral sex, and that's something I'm used to getting. I know you said you didn't feel comfortable doing it because it seemed lustful and dirty. But the truth is, God doesn't have a problem with anything sexual as long as it's done between a man and his wife."

"I know you keep saying that, but I need more time, Curtis."

"How *much* more time, baby, because I've already given you six months. I mean, how much longer am I going to have to wait for something I've never had to go without?"

"I promise you I'm going to do it very soon."

"You don't seem to have a problem when I do it for you," he said matter-of-factly.

"But it's not like I ask you to do it or like it's required."

"But I can tell that you love it, and not once can I remember you turning it down."

Mariah didn't respond, because she knew he was right. She never, ever turned it down. But even though she enjoyed it, she still felt as though it was somehow unnatural and morally wrong. Especially since Curtis always turned into a ravenous animal whenever they arrived at that point of their lovemaking. He seemed to be obsessed with doing that to her, and it was almost as if he enjoyed it more than she did. But regardless, she just didn't feel comfortable doing it for him.

"Curtis, honey, I know you really want this, but I don't think it's right. I mean, why can't we make love to each other without doing all of that?"

"Because, I want more than just regular intercourse. I *need* so much more than that. And at some point you're going to have to get over this squeamish mentality," he said, turning his head away from her.

"I know, Curtis. And I promise you, I'm going to pray about this every day until God gives me the strength to do it."

"*Pray?*" he said, wrinkling his forehead. "As far as I'm concerned, there's nothing to pray about. Either you're going to do it or you're not. But I'm telling you, if I don't get it soon, I can't be responsible—"

"You can't be responsible for what?" she interrupted.

"Nothing. I didn't mean anything at all. And hey, why don't we just forget about making love altogether," he said, and stood up.

"Okay, Curtis. I'll do it."

"No, that's okay, because I don't want you doing something just for the sake of doing it."

"It won't be like that. I promise. I mean, I've never done anything like this before, but I'm willing to try."

Curtis removed every stitch of clothing he was wearing and stepped in front of her. "It won't be as bad as you think."

Mariah didn't know how she should respond, so she didn't.

"And, baby?" he said.

"Yes," she answered, wondering how she was going to get through this.

"I want you to know that even though I already love you more than anything in this world, I'll love you even more after tonight. I'll love you in a way that you can't even imagine. Our marriage will rise to a whole new level, because we will have finally bonded completely."

"I love you, too, Curtis," Mariah said, and realized that this truly was important to her husband, and that his love for her was all that really mattered. She decided that as his wife, it was her job to keep him happy.

It was her job to keep him faithful.

Chapter 2

Curtis leaned back in his tall black executive-style chair and spun himself toward the window of his church study. It was hard to believe that even after the blackmail fiasco and total scandalizing of his name, he'd still been able to reenter the ministry as pastor of an equally prominent Baptist church. As a matter of fact, Truth Missionary Baptist Church now had over thirty-five hundred members on the rolls, which was five hundred more than they'd had at Faith, and they were now holding two morning services. One at eight and one at ten forty-five. Nine months ago, when he'd first become their pastor, they'd only had maybe thirty-two hundred, and that meant he was the reason they now had three hundred more. The board of deacons was very happy with the work he'd been doing thus far, and so was the congregation. He'd learned a long time ago that most people liked having a great leader and wanted to be told what to do. They didn't seem to mind following a strong, charismatic, intelligent man, and he was glad that God had blessed him with all three qualities. When he was married to Tanya, she'd thought he was full of himself whenever he took charge and told the congregation what to do. She despised when he told them how much money they should give. But he never listened to her because he knew that most people didn't always know what was best and sometimes needed a little direction. Sometimes they needed to have certain requests explained to them in a certain kind of way. Which was why he was now a lot more subtle when he made an appeal to the congregation. Which was why he was going to play Mr. Mild Mannered when he met with the deacons one week from today. He wasn't sure how they were going to feel about some of his new ideas, but he wasn't going to fly off the handle the way he always did with his former board. Sometimes they'd disagreed with him on every point, and Deacon Jackson, Adrienne's husband, had been the ring leader. The man had debated every idea Curtis suggested, but what the deacon didn't know was that Curtis was back. He hadn't seen the deacon in years, and had no idea what church he belonged to, but the joke was still going to be on him. Curtis was going to make sure of it.

When the phone rang, he flinched and returned to reality. Finally, he pressed the speaker button.

"Yes," he said.

"Pastor, if you have some time right now, I'd like to start working on your agenda for the deacon board meeting next week," Whitney said.

"Sure, that'll be fine, just give me a minute to finish writing some notes for you."

"Sounds good," she said, and hung up.

Whitney was Curtis's new executive assistant. She'd been working for the church for two years as a clerk-typist, but when Curtis decided he didn't want the same assistant the former pastor had hired, he told the woman that things weren't working out, and that he would give her a recommendation for any job she applied for outside of the church. Curtis hadn't liked her from the start, because there just hadn't been any chemistry between them. Plus, she reminded him of Monique, his former secretary. She was sorely unattractive, and constantly acted as if she was trying to come on to him. So Curtis spoke to the deacons, and although there was some uncertainty on their part, they allowed him to replace her.

And he was glad he did, because Whitney was every pastor's dream. She was young, beautiful, and extremely organized. She loved her job, and she loved her pastor. The only downfall was that she loved her husband, and hadn't hesitated to make sure Curtis knew it. The very first day she was promoted, she'd marched right into his office, closed his door, and sat down in front of him. She'd caught him completely off guard, and before he could speak, she told him, "I do phones, I do meetings, and I do travel arrangements, but I don't do pastors. And if you agree with all of that, then you and I will get along like best friends." Curtis had laughed almost immediately, but Whitney never cracked a smile. So after a few seconds, Curtis told her that he was fine with all of the above. Just thinking about the whole scenario made him smile, but he had to admit he'd had the highest respect for her ever since.

Curtis heard a knock at the door and told Whitney to come in.

"How's your afternoon going?" she said, walking in. She was dressed in a black microfiber ankle-length dress.

"Actually, my whole day has been going great. Now all I have to do is convince the deacons that it's time for us to use more modern methods and technology when it comes to the way tithes and offerings are paid. Here's some of my ideas," he said, passing Whitney a list he'd been compiling for a while now. She scanned it and shook her head.

"What?" Curtis asked.

"No, don't get me wrong. I understand each and every one of

your points, but I can already tell you right now that you're going to meet opposition from Deacon Thurgood and Deacon Winslow."

"Hmmm," Curtis said, clasping his hands together. "The two oldest deacons on the board, huh?"

"Yep. They're extremely old-school, and they don't like anything that sounds like a scam."

"But I'm not proposing anything like that."

"I totally agree, but I'm just letting you know how they'll see it."

"How did they end up on the board anyway, because most of the deacons that came over from Faith are much younger."

"They came from the church where Pastor Jenkins used to be an associate minister," she said, referring to their former pastor.

"Well, I wish they had stayed where they were, because I'm trying to move this church in an upward direction, and we can't do that if we keep doing things the same as they've always been done. I used to tell my old congregation that we have little because we think little, and I still feel the same way right now."

"Maybe if you can prove in laymen's terms that you're not trying to run a scam and that your ideas will benefit the church as a whole, maybe they'll understand."

"Maybe. But then who's to say? But I guess we'll see soon enough."

"I'll get everything typed up, though, and you can give me any additions as the week goes on."

"Well, now that we have that taken care of, what's going on with my preanniversary committee?" Curtis winked at her. "You know it's only three months away."

"You should be ashamed of yourself," Whitney said, smiling.

"I know, but can you blame me for being curious? I mean, that's going to be a very special day. Especially since the last anniversary celebration I had at Faith was the reason my preaching career ended." He didn't talk about that particular incident to very many people, but he confided just about everything to Whitney.

"I understand. So if you must know, they're planning a monthlong celebration with a different program each Sunday afternoon. They're also planning one full week of evening services right before the actual anniversary weekend."

The services were fine and necessary, but Curtis wanted to know about the gifts—specifically the monetary ones.

"Also," Whitney continued, "each member of the church will be asked to give one hundred dollars and no less than fifty. In addition to that, you'll be receiving all moneys collected at each of the precelebration services."

"What a blessing," Curtis said, but he wished they weren't planning to offer an option where people could pay fifty dollars. Some of them wouldn't even consider paying the maximum once they learned that half of it was acceptable. If only the committee realized that it was better to give the congregation one specific amount with no alternatives, because when they had too many choices, it sometimes confused their way of thinking. Although even if only one thousand of his members gave a hundred dollars, he'd still walk away with six figures.

"Yes, it really is," Whitney agreed.

"Excuse me?" Curtis asked. He'd become so enthralled with what the committee was planning to do, he'd forgotten what he and Whitney were discussing.

"I was just agreeing with you," she explained. "I was saying that all of this really is a blessing."

"That it is," Curtis added.

"Well, unless you have something else, I'd better get back out to my desk."

"No, I think that's it, and I'll let you know if I have anything to add to the agenda."

"Sounds good. Oh, and there is one other thing. I shouldn't be telling you this, but if I don't, you'll probably book your calendar so far in advance you won't be able to take advantage of the trip."

"What trip is that?"

"That's the other anniversary gift. The church is giving you and Mariah an all-expense-paid trip to anywhere you want to go."

"Wow. Now, that's a gift and then some."

"Just thought I'd let you know, but it would be nice if you didn't tell Mariah. That way, at least *someone* will be surprised when it's announced."

"Your secret is safe with me," he said as Whitney walked out and shut the door behind her.

An all-expense-paid trip with Mariah was never going to happen. She was boring him to pieces right here at home, so he couldn't possibly imagine being tied down on some tropical island with her. He'd hoped her giving him oral sex was going to make their sex lives a bit more interesting, but she just didn't know what she was doing. It was only her first time, but Curtis had already decided that she just didn't have what it took to satisfy him. She didn't have any of the sexual skills that any of his former women possessed. She wasn't Adrienne Jackson.

He'd seen Adrienne at a church concert a couple of weeks ago, but he'd made sure not to approach her because he hadn't wanted to stir up any old feelings. The truth: he hadn't wanted to be unfaithful to his new wife after only six months of marriage. He'd decided that he was going to do the right thing this time, no matter what. And he would have, if only Mariah had given him what he needed—if only she'd given him what he had to have in order to survive as a man. He'd stared at Adrienne on and off at the concert for two full hours, but he'd pushed the thought of calling her completely out of his system. He'd tried to forget about how good she'd once made him feel and how willing she was to do whatever he wanted. Anytime, anywhere. But six long months of nothing was long enough. As a matter of fact, it was too long, and it was time for him to do something about it. He wished there was another way, but right now he couldn't think of one.

Curtis dialed Adrienne's work number from memory, as if he'd just phoned her yesterday. There were some things a person simply didn't forget.

"This is Adrienne Jackson speaking," she answered.

"Adrienne. It's me."

There was a pause.

"Are you there?" Curtis asked.

"I'm here. Just a little surprised to hear your voice."

"I know. But to be honest, I haven't been able to get you off of my mind ever since I saw you."

"But you're married again, right?"

"Yes, but—"

"But nothing, Curtis. I mean, there is no but if you're married."

"Okay, okay. You're right. I am remarried, but I'm not happy. We've been together for six months, but I'm starting to realize it was a mistake."

Adrienne laughed at him.

"What's funny?"

"You."

"Why am I funny?"

"You're funny, Curtis, because after all this time you still haven't changed one bit."

"You're right. Because I certainly haven't changed when it comes to the way I feel about you."

"You know, I don't even want to hear it. And if that's what

you called to talk about, then we should end this conversation right now."

"I'm just being honest. I know I made a lot of mistakes in the past, and that I didn't do right by you, but I've been sorry for that ever since."

"Well, I'm sorry, too. I'm sorry that I ever met you, and that I allowed you to make such a fool of me. Do you know how humiliating it was for me to have Thomas find out about that abortion, the condo that you and I were renting, and then have him tell the entire congregation everything he knew about you and me? I mean everything, Curtis. He didn't leave out one thing."

"I know, I know, I know. I was just as humiliated as you were. Even more, if you want to know the truth."

"Well, you got what you deserved."

"So did you and the deacon end up getting divorced?" Curtis said, changing the subject.

"First of all, he's not a deacon anymore, and he hasn't stepped foot inside a church ever since that terrible day five years ago. And to answer your question, no, we didn't get divorced. He did put me out because of you, but after I begged him for almost a year, he finally took me back, and we've been doing great ever since."

"Come on now, Adrienne. This is me you're talking to. You can't be doing that great, because you know you don't love him."

"How in the hell would you know?" she said, and Curtis heard a door shut, probably the one to her office.

"I know because you *never* loved him. You never even loved him before you met me."

"You don't know what you're talking about, and I really don't have time for this."

"I'm just calling things the way I see them, but I'm not trying to offend you."

"Well, I have to go."

"Can I see you?"

"Didn't you hear me say that Thomas and I are still married?"

"Yes, but, Adrienne, all I want to do is talk to you. We can even meet at a restaurant downtown if you want."

"No."

"Adrienne, baby. Don't you remember how good we were together? Don't you remember all the good times we had and how unbelievable our lovemaking was? And can you honestly tell me that the deacon is giving you half of what I gave you in bed? I know Mariah hasn't even come close to satisfying me the way you always did, and I can't take it anymore. I miss being with you, Adrienne. I miss everything about you."

"Curtis, I can't do this again. I can't."

"Just meet me this one time, and if you decide you don't ever want to see me again, I'll back off completely."

"You used me all those months, and then you just dropped me. I mean, how could you be so cruel if you loved me the way you kept claiming?"

"I was totally messed up in the head back then. I was so overwhelmed with my responsibilities at the church, I was miserable with Tanya, and the deacons and I were at each other's throats constantly. And I'll admit I shouldn't have gotten myself involved with those other women when you were all I ever needed."

"Women like who? That girl Charlotte, who had your baby? Or was it the two women you were caught on videotape with?"

Curtis wondered how she knew about the tape, since he'd been told that the deacons hadn't received it until after Deacon Jackson was suspended from the board. But he was sure the news had still traveled pretty quickly by word of mouth. He still remembered all the gossipy women who attended Faith and how they were constantly in his business. But the strangest part of all was that Mariah lived right here in Chicago, too, but hadn't heard one word about his past indiscretions. What she didn't know, though, couldn't hurt her, and her ignorance was for the best.

"Look," he finally said. "Let's not talk about anyone except you and me. Okay?"

"Do you realize how much I loved you and how much I hurt my husband because of it? Do you know how hurt I was when you told me our relationship was over and that I needed to move on? Do you?"

"I know, and I'm willing to try and make that up to you. If only you would meet me for dinner, I'd be able to explain things so much better. I know you're angry because of how things turned out, but if you'll just give me a chance to talk to you."

Adrienne was silent.

"Baby, please. I promise you I'll make it worth your while. If nothing else, our meeting will give us some much needed closure."

"It's not right. And the last thing I want to do is hurt Thomas all over again. You and I did a serious job of that five years ago, and I'll never forgive myself for that."

"He doesn't have to know about one little dinner, does he?"

"I don't even want to take the chance of having him find out."

"I don't just want to see you, Adrienne, I need to see you. I need to see you face-to-face."

"Curtis, why are you doing this?"

Her feathers were finally beginning to ruffle.

"I'm doing it because I'm still in love with you. I've tried hard to forget about you, but I can't. Just one innocent meeting. That's all I'm asking."

"Where?"

"What about the place I took you to when you got that promotion?"

"When?"

"Tonight at six."

"I'll meet you for dinner, but that's it."

"Fine."

"I'm serious, Curtis. That's as far as I'm going."

"I hear you loud and clear."

"Bye," she said, and hung up.

Curtis called the Hyatt to see if they had any last-minute vacancies. He told the 800 operator that any Chicago suburb would do.

Chapter 3

ook, sweetheart," Curtis said to Mariah from his cell phone while pulling his black Escalade into a parking ramp on Wacker Street. "How was I supposed to know that you were cooking me a surprise dinner? I mean if I'd known before now, I wouldn't have committed to this regional ministers' meeting."

Mariah's silence confirmed her disappointment, but Curtis wasn't about to change his plans with Adrienne. He felt sorry for Mariah, but there was nothing he could do about it now.

"Why don't you invite your mother and sisters over? It's not like you ever spend that much time with them, anyway," he said. Although, truthfully, he couldn't have cared less whether they ever visited, because they were much too classless and ghetto.

"I only cooked enough for two," she said.

"Then maybe you could just invite your mother."

"We'll see."

"I'm really sorry, baby, but I promise I'll be home as soon as the meeting is over."

"Fine, Curtis."

"Mariah, I really am sorry about this."

"I said I was fine, didn't I?"

"Whoa. Am I sensing a little bit of irritation here?"

"No. But I'm really disappointed, because I spent all day preparing this meal for you. Macaroni and cheese, baked beans, smothered ribs. I even made you that carrot cake you love so much."

"Well, I said I was sorry, so I'm not sure what else you expect me to do. Unless you want me to ignore my pastoral obligations just so I can come home and be with you."

"No, no, no. That's not what I mean. It's just that I wanted so much for us to spend the evening together."

"I understand that, baby, and we will as soon as I get home."

"I'll be waiting for you."

"See you in a few hours."

"And Curtis?"

"Yeah?"

"I love you."

"I love you, too, baby."

Curtis pressed the On-Star button inside the rearview mirror and ended his call to Mariah. He blew a sigh of frustration and relief. He was happy that Mariah never nagged him the way Tanya always had, but irritated because she always wanted him to spend so much time with her. With the exception of Bible study, other church-related events, and shopping, she didn't like doing much else without him. But starting tonight, she was going to have to end this clinginess and find other interests. She would have to find other ways to occupy her time, because if things went the way he was expecting, he would soon be spending a whole lot more time with Adrienne.

Curtis tossed Mariah out of his mind and maneuvered into a parking stall. Adrienne pulled up next to him in a white Mercedes. Her hair hung freely just past her shoulder blades, just the way he liked it.

He smiled at her, stepped outside of his car, and set the alarm system.

"I see you're still looking as gorgeous as ever," he complimented her.

"Really? Well, you're not."

Curtis laughed. "Okay, I guess I deserve that," he said as they walked toward the restaurant.

"Yes, Curtis, you do deserve that . . . and so much more. Which is why I never should have come down here in the first place."

"You came because you knew it was the right thing to do, and because deep down you know you still care about me."

Adrienne looked around to see if anyone was walking behind them, listening to their conversation.

"This just isn't right," she said matter-of-factly.

When they arrived in front of the restaurant, Curtis opened the door and waited for Adrienne to walk through it. Once inside, Curtis told the maître d' that they had a reservation.

"Right this way, Mr. Black," the slender forty-something man said, and then escorted them to a candlelit circular booth. "Your waitress will be with you momentarily."

"Thank you," Curtis offered.

"So what is it that you wanted to talk to me about?" Adrienne asked almost immediately.

"Us. And I wanted to tell you how sorry I am for causing you so much pain. I must have been completely out of my mind to end our relationship the way I did."

"Hmmph. Well, that's all in the past now, isn't it? So I ask you again, what did you want to talk to me about?"

"You're not going to make this easy, are you?" he said, smiling.

"No, I'm not. Because you treated me like I was nothing—like what we had never mattered to you in the least."

"Now, baby, you know that's not true. What you and I had was special, and I've never been more comfortable with any woman than I was with you. It's just that I got myself caught up in that terrible marriage to Tanya and couldn't see my way out of it without losing the church."

"But you lost it anyway, so what difference did it make?"

"I know, and I've regretted not staying with you ever since. You can't imagine how much."

A very thin woman in her late twenties sat two glasses of water down on the table. "What can I get you to drink?"

"I'll have some brandy," Adrienne answered.

Curtis looked at her in shock, but her eyes dared him to comment.

"I'll have a Perrier with lime," he said.

"Can I bring either of you an appetizer?"

"I'll have a small Caesar salad," Adrienne said.

"I'll have the field greens with vinaigrette," Curtis added.

"Sounds good. I'll bring them right out."

"So when did you start drinking hard liquor?" Curtis wanted to know.

"When? I'll tell you when. It was right around the time your little lying ass decided to dump me," Adrienne spat out.

Curtis stared at her.

"Was that a good enough answer for you, Reverend Curtis Black?"

"Not really, because I still can't believe you're drinking alcohol."

"Why, because it's not Christian-like?"

"Well, now that you bring it up, yes. Because you know very well how sinful it is to drink intoxicating beverages."

Adrienne laughed louder than Curtis would have liked, because people were starting to look in their direction.

"Did I say something funny?" he asked.

"Everything about you is funny. As a matter of fact, you're

the biggest joke I know. Because how in the world can you sit there and judge my drinking when just five years ago you were screwing my brains out every chance you got. And this was all while you were married to Tanya. Not to mention the fact that you have another wife at home right now, but still you're sitting here with me."

"None of us falls short of sin, Adrienne. We all make mistakes."

"Whatever."

It was time to change the subject. "So you say you and the deacon are happily married, huh?"

"Didn't I tell you that he's no longer a deacon?"

Curtis smiled at Adrienne. He'd heard what she said, but *Thomas*, as she referred to him, would always be *the deacon* in Curtis's book, because Curtis liked the way it sounded. He loved the sarcasm of it.

"He'll always be the deacon to me," Curtis said.

"Whatever."

"So?"

"So what?" Adrienne was irritated.

"Are you and the deacon happily married?"

"Yes. *Very* happy."

"If you say so."

"I do," she said, and looked the other way.

Curtis was finally starting to realize that Adrienne wasn't coming back to him without a fight. It was time to do and say whatever it would take to win her over, so he leaned against the leather backrest and clasped his hands together on top of the table. "You know, baby, it would be so much easier if you would at least *try* to forgive me. I know I was wrong for all the pain I caused you, but I'm willing to spend the rest of my life making things up to you. I don't love Mariah, and it's only going to be a matter of time before I ask her for a divorce. She can't do for me what you can. She can't make me feel the way you can. And now that I'm sitting here with you, I realize how much I'm still in love with you. I knew my feelings for you were still strong, but I didn't know that being this close to you would trigger my heart the way it has. I know you don't believe me, but I don't just *want* you back in my life, I desperately need you," he said, gently grabbing her hand.

Adrienne's face softened, but not enough for him to tell what she was thinking.

"Do you hear what I'm saying, baby? I need you to come back to me, because I don't think I can live without you any longer."

"Then why did you marry someone else, Curtis? Why did you do that?"

The waitress returned with their drinks, salads, and a basket of rolls. Then she jotted down their lobster and shrimp orders and left again.

"I don't know why. I guess I didn't think you would ever take me back, and to be honest, I thought it would be better if I left my past exactly where it was. I really wanted to start things right at this new church. And everything might've worked fine, except Mariah doesn't satisfy me. We've only been married for a short while, but I don't love her nearly the way a husband should love his wife. I don't love her nearly as much as I love you."

"I can't do this, Curtis. I can't do this to Thomas, and I won't allow you to hurt me all over again. What we did back then was wrong, and God won't forget that," she said, picking up her brandy.

Curtis reached for her glass. "Adrienne, please don't."

"Why? It's just one drink."

"Because you don't need it and because it's so ungodly. And you know how much that sort of thing turns me off. I can't stand to see any woman drink, smoke, or do drugs."

"Why are you trying to control me, Curtis?" she said, lifting a forkful of salad.

"Baby, I'm not. Our bodies are sacred, and you know as well as I do that it's a sin to harm what God has created," he said, chewing some of his mixed greens.

"Whatever you say."

"So, are you going to forgive me?"

"I don't know. I just don't think I'll ever be able to do that."

"Well, you know what the scripture says. 'Forgive us our trespasses as we forgive those who trespass against us.' And you can't get into heaven if you don't learn to forgive people."

"We won't get into heaven by committing adultery either. I knew it when I first started sleeping with you, and I still know it now. Because it's not like some sins are okay to commit and some aren't. A sin is a sin is a sin, and there's no denying that."

"That's true, but God knows that we are not perfect, and that we are sometimes too weak to ignore certain temptations. It's different for everybody. Some people like to steal, some people like using the Lord's name in vain, and some people use vulgarity and excessive anger on a regular basis. For you and me, it's adultery. I keep telling you that none of us falls short and we have to pray constantly, asking for forgiveness."

"And I've always told you that God doesn't look favorably on people who knowingly commit sins just because they know they can ask for forgiveness later."

"You're making all this much more complicated than it needs to be. Because the bottom line is that I'm in love with you and, right or wrong, I can't do anything to change that."

"But you're married to someone else, Curtis. You could have easily looked me up after you and Tanya were divorced, but you never even tried."

"I know. And I'll regret that for the rest of my life. But it won't always be this way, because I'm not going to stay married to Mariah."

"Really now? And when exactly are you planning to divorce this particular wife?"

"Soon. But I at least have to stay married to her for a year so it doesn't look bad to the deacons or the congregation."

"Oh no, here we go. Have you forgotten the fact that you told me that same lie when you were married to Tanya?"

"I know, but this is different. I promise you that it will only be six more months, tops."

"Two lobster and shrimp specials," the waitress said, sitting the plates down on the table. "Can I get you anything else?"

"No, I think we're fine for now," Curtis said.

"Yes, everything is fine," Adrienne added.

"Enjoy your meals."

Curtis and Adrienne managed to make conversation while finishing dinner and then left the restaurant. When they arrived in the parking garage, Curtis opened Adrienne's car door for her.

"Well, it was good to see——" she began, but Curtis kissed her mid-sentence.

"Curtis, don't," she said, pulling away from him.

He gently stroked her face. "Adrienne. Baby, please. Just give me this one last chance, and I promise I'll do right by you."

"No, Curtis. Please just go," she said.

He pulled her toward him and kissed her again. This time her resistance was less physical, and Curtis could tell that there was still a great deal of fire and passion between them. It felt as though they'd never been apart.

But she jerked away from him.

"Curtis, I told you that I won't do this again, and I want you to leave me alone for good."

"But, baby," he said, pleading.

"No," she said flatly. "I mean it, Curtis. Don't call me and don't try to see me."

"I can't believe you're doing this. Not after all we've been through together. Not after seeing me again and realizing that we still love each other."

Adrienne shook her head, frustrated by his persistence.

"Please, just let me go, Curtis. Please."

Curtis hesitated but then stepped away. Adrienne sat in her car, shut the door, and backed the car away from him. She never looked back, and Curtis wondered what he was going to have to do to change her mind. He wondered how many more phone calls he'd have to make and how many dozens of flowers he'd have to send. Maybe jewelry would do the trick. He wasn't sure what it was going to take, but the one thing he did know was that he needed her in his life again. He needed her more than ever before.

"I don't know, Vivian," Mariah said to her best friend after phoning her a half hour ago. "I guess I'm just feeling a bit uneasy because tonight is the first time he called at the last minute to say he wouldn't be home for dinner. It was so unlike him not to have told me that earlier in the day."

"I hear what you're saying, girl, but he is a very well-known pastor. So I'm sure there are going to be many days when he'll forget to tell you about certain meetings."

"You're right, but it still bothered me. Not to mention it's almost nine and he's still not home yet."

"Maybe they sat around laughing and talking once the meeting was over. Because I'm sure they don't spend all their time discussing just the Bible and what's going on at their churches. I would think they have to socialize at least sometimes."

"Maybe."

"Girl, you have a wonderful man who loves and takes care of
you, so stop your worrying. As a matter of fact, I remember you
praying that Curtis would eventually be your husband, so I
think you need to keep an open mind and just be thankful for
what God has given you."

"I am thankful, and I do know that he's a good man, but . . .
you know what, I think that's him coming in right now."

"See, I told you. Now get off this phone and go greet that
man like a good wife ought to."

"Talk to you later."

"Have fun."

Mariah walked downstairs and saw Curtis removing his
blazer.

"So how was the meeting?" she asked, kissing him.

"It was lengthy as usual, but productive. We met until
around eight and then I stopped at a deli to get a sandwich. So
that's why I'm just now getting home."

"Oh. Well then, I guess you're not hungry."

"No, I'm not. And I'm sorry I didn't make it home for dinner. But what you can do is warm everything up tomorrow
when Alicia gets here," he said, referring to his daughter.

"Fine," Mariah said, dreading her stepdaughter's visit. Not
because she didn't like Alicia, but because Alicia always made
Mariah feel like an intrusion. Curtis kept insisting that things
would get better, but they hadn't. It was the same routine every
other weekend. Alicia would walk into the house, speak to
Mariah with no enthusiasm, and then head up to her bedroom.
Mariah was trying to be patient with her, since she'd only been
her stepmother for a few months, but she was beginning to run
out of ways to get on her good side. She hoped this weekend
would be different.

"I'm beat," Curtis said, stretching. "Let's head up to bed."

"And do what?" Mariah teased him.

"Fall into a very deep sleep."

"What about before that?" she said, walking up the winding staircase in front of him.

"Not tonight, baby. I'm really tired, and I have to get up pretty early in the morning."

Mariah felt her stomach stirring. This was definitely a first. Curtis coming home on any day of the week and not wanting to make love to her? She wanted to ask him what was wrong, but decided against it because she didn't want to sound suspicious. Maybe he didn't want her because he was tired of begging for oral sex. He'd said he couldn't be responsible for what might happen if he didn't get what he needed, and that's why she'd done the best she could yesterday afternoon. But she knew with everything inside her that she hadn't satisfied him. He'd told her it was good, but his facial expression screamed another story. She wanted to get better at it and was willing to practice until she was perfect.

When they entered the master bedroom suite, Mariah pulled him toward her and kissed him. They kissed until Curtis pulled away and began removing his clothing. But Mariah wasn't giving up so easily. She wasn't about to let him drop off to sleep before giving him what he swore he needed.

"Sweetheart, let me do something special for you."

"Mariah, honey. I'm really, really tired. But I promise you we'll make love tomorrow."

She heard every word he said, but ignored his wishes. She slid his underwear down to the floor and rested her weight on her knees. Curtis watched her but didn't move. Mariah massaged him and then took him inside her mouth. She tried to pleasure him the exact same way she'd seen some woman pleasure her husband on one of the pay channels. She'd been flipping through them just before calling Vivian and decided to see how this was supposed to be done. She still thought it was unnatural and deplored it, but believed it was her duty to keep Curtis happy.

Mariah hoped she was doing it right this time, and when she saw Curtis's eyes roll toward the back of his head, she knew she was on track. She would only get better as time went on, and then he wouldn't have a single thing to complain about. There would be no reason at all why he'd ever consider going astray. She realized that Vivian was right. There wasn't anything at all she should be worrying about when it came to Curtis.

Chapter 4

Alicia packed her overnight bag and wished she could spend the weekend with her father without his new wife. Mariah was a nice enough woman, but Alicia longed for the time she and her father used to spend alone. Even more, she wanted her father and mother to tell their current spouses that things just weren't working out, and that they'd decided to remarry. Then maybe Alicia and her parents could finally get back to the happily-ever-after they once lived. But she knew it was all wishful thinking because her mother couldn't have been happier with James and her father seemed to be fairly happy with Mariah.

"Alicia, are you ready?" she heard her mother ask.

"Yes, Mom, I'm coming."

"We need to get going because I told Mariah that I'd have you over there in time for dinner."

Alicia showed no concern but gathered up her bag and portable CD player. When she went downstairs, she saw her stepfather smiling at her.

"Have a good time, pumpkin," James said.

"I'll try," she said, forcing a positive attitude.

As Tanya and Alicia drove out of the subdivision, Alicia noticed her best friend getting in the car with her parents and waved at them.

"How come you and Daddy couldn't be as happy as Danielle's parents?"

"Every marriage doesn't work out that way."

"Well, why did you and Daddy get married if you weren't going to stay together?"

"Now, Alicia, we've been through this over and over again for the last five years," Tanya explained. "You know the reason why your father and I ended up getting a divorce."

"Oh yeah, I forgot. Daddy slept with practically every woman at the church."

"Alicia! You know that's not true."

"It might as well be, because what difference does it make if he slept with three women or three hundred. Either way, he was wrong and he broke up our family."

"But he's still your father, and it's time for you to try and forgive him. We've both moved on with our lives, and while I know it's been very difficult for you, you're going to have to accept it."

"I have forgiven him. And everything was just fine until he had to go and marry Mariah. It's just not fair."

"I understand how you feel, but Mariah is his wife. And I want you to start giving her much more respect than you have been."

Alicia turned to look at her mother. "Who said I don't give her respect?"

"Your father told me that you never hold a decent conversation with her and that most of the time you only answer questions."

Alicia wished her father would spend more time being a better father and less time reporting what she was or wasn't doing.

He made her so sick sometimes. It was bad enough that he'd ruined her life when she was nine and now he was trying to do the same thing at fourteen. She was practically grown, and she wondered when he was going to stop treating her like a baby. She wondered when both he and her mother were going to realize that she had her own life to live and that they should simply worry about themselves.

"Why should I talk to her when I really don't know who she is?"

Tanya turned onto Curtis's street. "But that's how you could get to know her. If you don't talk to people, how do you ever expect to build a relationship with them?"

Hmmph, Alicia thought. What her mother didn't know was that she didn't want a relationship with her father's wife. What she wanted was for Mariah to move out of the way or, better yet, go back to wherever she came from.

Alicia didn't respond to her mother's latest comment, and before long Tanya pulled up the circle driveway and stopped in front of her ex-husband's new living quarters. The off-white stucco was gorgeous and the landscaping was immaculate.

Alicia noticed her mother admiring the house. "Don't you wish this was your home instead of Mariah's? I mean, look at it, Mom. It's even bigger than the one we used to live in."

"No, Alicia. I don't wish this was my house. I'm very happy with the house that James and I have, and I'm very happy for your father and Mariah."

"But why? I mean, how can you be happy for a man who treated you like Daddy did?"

"Look, Alicia. That's enough. And instead of discussing grown folks' business, I think you need to spend your time worrying about that failing progress report you brought home yesterday."

Alicia sighed strongly. "Bye," she said, stepping onto the pavement.

"You'd better get rid of that little attitude, Alicia," Tanya yelled.

Alicia glanced back at her mother and then slammed the door behind her.

Tanya got out of the vehicle and followed Alicia. "Girl, have you lost your natural mind? You must think I'm a kid or some-thin'."

Mariah opened the door. "Hi, Alicia. Hi, Tanya."

"How are you, Mariah?" Tanya asked.

"I'm fine. Do you want to come in for a few minutes?"

"No, I really have to get going. And, Alicia, you'd better straighten up that face of yours."

Alicia kept pouting.

"What's going on?" Curtis asked, walking toward them.

"Nothing," Alicia answered nonchalantly.

"Curtis, you had better have a long talk with your daughter, otherwise she's going to see a side of me she's never seen be-fore," Tanya said. "This attitude of hers has got to go, because I'm not about to keep putting up with her smart little mouth. And before I forget, I think you should know that she brought home a failing progress report from world history yesterday."

"Alicia? Failing a class?" Curtis commented.

"Yes, and something has got to be done about it," Tanya said, turning to walk back to her car. "Oh, and, Mariah, it was good seeing you again."

"You too, Tanya."

Mariah closed the door, and Tanya drove off.

"Alicia, what is this all about?" Curtis asked.

"Nothing," she repeated.

"Well, it must be *something*, because gifted students who have always gotten straight A's don't bring home failing progress reports."

Alicia gazed into thin air and wished they would all drop

dead. Or maybe it would be better if she died herself. She was so tired of them telling her what she needed to do and sick of them harassing her.

"Girl, do you hear me talking to you?" Curtis said.

"Yes."

"Then you'd better act like it. Now I'm going to ask you again. What is this all about?"

"It's about you and the way you broke up our family. It's about you and how you slept with Deacon Jackson's wife behind Mom's back. It's about that girl Charlotte that you got pregnant. And it's also about you getting married and not spending any real time with me. That's what this is all about, Daddy. It's all about you," she screamed, with tears flooding her face.

Mariah was speechless.

Curtis had no sympathy.

"Alicia, what I want you to do is go up to your room and stay there until I tell you to come out."

Alicia stormed upstairs and slammed her bedroom door. She heard her father and Mariah conversing and wished she hadn't even come for this visit. She hated all of them. Her father, Mariah, and even her mother at this particular moment. This was her first year in high school, and they were doing everything they could to ruin it. So what if she *had* brought home a less than average progress report? It was the first time ever, and it certainly didn't compare to all the horrible things her father had done. That was for sure. So why couldn't they just mind their own business and leave her alone? It wasn't like they really cared about her, anyway. She didn't have one person she could turn to, and she was starting to wonder more and more why she even hung around. Maybe they would all be happier if she disappeared. Maybe then they'd realize what terrible parents they were and that her unhappiness was all their fault.

She lay across her bed, crying silently. She wished she could be nine again. That way, she would stop her father from ever cheating on her mother. That way, the three of them would be together again and she could continue being the happiest little girl in the world.

"Curtis, who is Charlotte?" Mariah asked.

"Baby, sit down," he said, barely looking at her.

"And what's this about you getting her pregnant?"

"She was a girl who attended Faith when I was pastor over there, and as wrong as it was, I had an affair with her."

"You what! How old was she?"

"She was seventeen when I started seeing her."

"Why didn't you tell me you had another child, Curtis?"

"Because I just didn't know how. I was afraid that you wouldn't marry me if you knew. But now I know that I had no right keeping this from you."

"Have you seen her since she had the baby?"

"No. I haven't."

"Is it a boy or girl?"

"It's a boy."

"Well, why haven't you seen him?"

"Because her parents said that if I ever came near her or the baby, they would press statutory rape charges against me."

"Dear God," Mariah said.

"Baby, I'm sorry. I know I should have told you. But it's not like my son will ever be a part of our lives."

"What else haven't you told me, Curtis? I feel so stupid."

"That's everything. I swear on my life. There are no more secrets."

Mariah's head started to pound, and she wanted to go lie down. She was having a hard time digesting any of what she'd just learned and was ashamed of what she was thinking. She almost despised the fact that two other women had given her husband something she hadn't. Tanya and Charlotte had given him his own flesh and blood, and there was only one way she could compete with that. But Curtis had made it clear from the start that he wanted to wait a while before they tried to have a baby.

"Mariah, I am truly, truly sorry for not telling you," Curtis said, holding her. "I was wrong, and I hope you can forgive me. I won't ever keep anything else from you for as long as I live."

She didn't know what to say. She wanted to respond to him, but she couldn't find the words. Her heart ached heavily, and regardless of what Curtis claimed, she wondered what other skeletons he might have dangling elsewhere. She wanted to believe in him, but this newfound information that Alicia had boldly disclosed was a major blow. It had shaken her entire thinking and caused her to wonder if Curtis really was the man he claimed to be.

"Baby, say something," Curtis pleaded.

"The thing is . . . I don't know what to say about any of this."

"You do know why this is happening, don't you?" he asked.

"No. I don't."

"Because Satan doesn't want to see us happy. He's been trying to tear me down ever since I answered my call to preach, and now he's at it again. But this time he's trying to attack you and me through my little girl. He knows how happy I am with you and how much I love my daughter, so that's why he's doing this. So, baby, please don't let him win. Please don't give him what he wants."

He released Mariah from his hold.

"Satan, you are a liar!" he yelled. "You've been trying to get me for years, but today I rebuke you in the name of Jesus. I want you out of my house and out of my life for good. You hear me? Get out of here and find someone else to mess with. I mean it. I want you out of here."

Curtis broke into tears and spoke in tongues.

He seemed so distraught and Mariah felt sorry for him. Alicia walked down the staircase to see what was going on, and Curtis grabbed her tightly.

"Oh Lord, I am so sorry for all the sins I've committed and for hurting so many innocent people. But, Father, I ask you, please protect my daughter and make Satan stop influencing her. Force him to leave us alone so that we can do Your will instead."

Alicia stepped away from her father. Then she walked back up to her room, totally unimpressed. Curtis kneeled down in front of Mariah.

"Baby, I'm sorry. Do you hear me? I'm so sorry I don't know what to do. I was wrong for committing adultery against Tanya and I was wrong for not telling you about my other child. But if I have to, I'll spend the rest of my life making everything up to you."

Mariah didn't bother responding, but deep down she knew she would never see her husband in the same light.

She knew their six-month honeymoon was officially over.

Alicia gazed around her weekend boudoir and wondered why her father was downstairs clowning like that. He always resorted to praising God and rebuking Satan whenever someone cornered him, and he always blamed the devil for every sin he committed. She loved her father, but she was at the point where she just didn't like him very much anymore. She'd been so disappointed in him that day Deacon Jackson stood in front of the congregation and told everyone what her father and Deacon Jackson's wife had been doing. She remembered how he'd said her father had paid for Mrs. Jackson to have an abortion. Alicia hadn't even known what an abortion was until one of her cousins explained it to her a year later. That whole pastor's anniversary fiasco was the reason she now refused to attend any of his church services. She'd only been to his new church once, and that was only because he begged her to come to his installation ceremony.

She was so tired of spending every other weekend with them, but the only reason she continued doing it was that she wanted Mariah to know she had a stepdaughter who would always be in the picture. She wanted her to know that she'd never have her husband strictly to herself if Alicia could help it.

Alicia rose from her bed and sat down in front of the flat-screen monitor on her desk. As of late, the Internet was her only outlet, and she hoped Julian was on-line to chat with her. She loved communicating with him, because he never judged her and always listened to whatever she had to say. He always understood what she was going through and knew exactly what to say to make her feel better. She'd never met him face-to-face, but it was if she'd known him for years and years. They'd only been chatting for two weeks, after meeting in a chat room for young, single Chicagoans, but he'd already said that he couldn't wait to meet her. He'd said that he wanted to spend some time with her because he could tell how wonderful she was. So maybe the time was finally right for them to get together.

She clicked the sign-on button and within two seconds the DSL took her to the AOL Welcome screen. The first thing she saw was a weight-loss promotion. Alicia wondered why there were always so many of them. Not just on-line but also on television. She especially didn't understand why it was so hard for people to lose weight, since she ate anything she wanted and never gained a pound. Although her mother insisted it was only because she was well under thirty.

Alicia checked her e-mail messages and answered the one from Nikki, one of her classmates. She'd told Julian that it was best he didn't e-mail her just in case her mother decided to snoop around her computer. So what they did was add each other to their buddy list. That way, they could see when the other signed on and could chat through the Instant Message feature.

She surfed a few web sites and was just about to sign off when she saw the letters "JMoney1" appear in the upper right-hand corner.

ALICIABLK: Hey, Julian.

JMONEY1: Hey, Alicia. What's up?

ALICIABLK: I was just about to sign off, but I'm glad I didn't.

JMONEY1: So where are you?

ALICIABLK: I'm at my dad's, but I'm sorry I came over here.

JMONEY1: Why is that?

ALICIABLK: Because my mother told him about this progress report I got and he started tripping out about it. But I also told him exactly what I thought of him and how he broke up our family.

JMONEY1: Uh-oh. I'm sorry to hear that.

ALICIABLK: It's not your fault, and I'm just glad you came on-line tonight.

JMONEY1: I've been thinking about you all day. I do that a lot lately.

ALICIABLK: I think about you a lot, too.

JMONEY1: So when am I going to finally get a chance to meet Ms. Alicia Black?

ALICIABLK: I don't know. When do you want to?

Alicia felt somewhat nervous after sending her last response, because even though she really wanted to see Julian, she couldn't dismiss the fact that he was nineteen, and five whole years older than her. She didn't even want to imagine what her parents would say if they ever found out about him. Worse, she wondered how angry Julian would be if he knew she wasn't seventeen like she'd told him. She hadn't meant to deceive him, but she hadn't wanted him thinking she was some pathetic little kid.

JMONEY1: It's on you. I'm available whenever you say you're ready.

ALICIABLK: I'll let you know, but I promise it will be very soon.

JMONEY1: You know I can't wait.

ALICIABLK: Neither can I.

JMONEY1: So what are you doing this weekend with your dad?

ALICIABLK: Who knows? I might ask my mom to come and get me in the morning, because I really don't want to be here with him or Mariah.

There was a longer than usual pause with Julian's response.

JMONEY1: Can I ask you something?

ALICIABLK: Yes.

JMONEY1: What is it that you don't like about your step-moms?

ALICIABLK: I don't like her because my father and I were so close before she came into the picture, and I can't stand how she caters to him. She's so stupid, and she goes along with whatever he says. My mother never did that.

JMONEY1: But is she nice to you?

ALICIABLK: Yeah. I guess.

JMONEY1: But you still don't like her, though?

ALICIABLK: I don't hate her if that's what you mean.

JMONEY1: You seem to like your stepdad, so why is that?

ALICIABLK: Because he loves me like a daughter and he

doesn't take away my time with my mom. And if it's okay, I don't want to talk about this any longer.

JMONEY1: Okay. I'm sorry. I didn't mean to upset you. I was only trying to help you adjust to your new stepmoms. My stepmoms treated me so much better than my own mother did, so that's why I wondered if yours was nice to you. My mother was an abusive drug addict and she never cared about my brother or me. My father wasn't the best person either, so my stepmoms was all we had to depend on.

ALICIABLK: She's okay, but right now I'm not feeling her. Maybe if she had a backbone and let me spend some time alone with my father, it would be different.

JMONEY1: Hey, can you sit tight for a minute?

ALICIABLK: Sure.

Alicia visited a few more web sites until she heard the Instant Message chime ten minutes later.

JMONEY1: Okay, I'm back. Sorry about that.

ALICIABLK: Julian, can I ask you something?

JMONEY1: Shoot.

ALICIABLK: Do you have a girlfriend?

JMONEY1: No. Why do you ask? Do you want to be that person?

ALICIABLK: ☺Actually, I was just wondering.

JMONEY1: Well, since we're on the subject, do you have a boyfriend?

ALICIABLK: No.

JMONEY1: Good. Because I wouldn't want to have to kick some dude's behind over you.

ALICIABLK: LOL. You are so crazy.

JMONEY1: So tell me, girl. When are we gonna get together?

ALICIABLK: I told you it'll be very soon . . . Maybe in a couple of weeks.

JMONEY1: If you say so.

ALICIABLK: I promise.

JMONEY1: Well, hey, I'm about to roll with one of my boys, but I'll be on again tomorrow night around the same time.

ALICIABLK: Talk to you then.

JMONEY1: Cya.

Alicia signed off the computer and heard Mariah calling her downstairs to dinner. Right now she wasn't even hungry and didn't have one word to say to her father. She certainly didn't want to sit at the table watching him pretend like he was the holiest man alive or listen to him beg Mariah for her forgiveness. Alicia had watched him manipulate people even before she knew what the word meant, and she was sick of it. She'd thought the world of him when she was much younger, but now she knew he was an impostor. She was only fourteen, but even she was old enough to know that her father was going to burn in hell if he didn't stop playing with God.

She decided that she wasn't going to spend another weekend with him for a very long time. Somehow it just didn't make sense to.

Chapter 5

Curtis switched the phone from one ear to the other. "Baby, I'm sorry to tell you this, but as soon as I finish meeting with the deacons and trustees, I have to go visit the Wilsons. I just found out this afternoon that they had a death in their family," he said to Mariah as carefully as he could. She wasn't going to stop him from doing whatever he wanted, but he could tell she hadn't been quite the same ever since Alicia blabbed about Charlotte and his son four days ago, and he didn't want her getting any crazy ideas. Ideas like leaving him and filing for a divorce. He didn't think she had it in her, but he couldn't take any chances. The last thing he wanted was to have to explain to the deacon board why another wife had left him.

"Curtis, what is going on? Last week you called me at the last minute saying you had a meeting, and last night you didn't make it home until after nine."

"But I already told you, Mariah. I was at the church working on next week's sermon."

"But you hardly ever work on Mondays."

"No, but yesterday I felt like working, so I did. I worked so I wouldn't have to work so hard on Thursday and Friday trying to prepare for Sunday."

"Curtis, I'm really getting worried."

"Worried about what?" He frowned.

"Us. Because I'm starting to feel like you don't want to spend time with me anymore."

He was trying to be patient and cordial, but she was starting to get on his nerves. She was starting to sound like Tanya all over again, and he wasn't going to tolerate it.

"Look, Mariah. I don't have the liberty of sitting at home with you all day or coming home every single evening right on schedule. I wish I could, but I can't. I have a church to run, and you're just going to have to understand that."

"I do understand, but ever since last week you've been different."

"Different how?" he asked, raising his voice.

"You seem distant and like you really don't want to touch me."

"Oh Lord. Not all these accusations again."

"What is that supposed to mean?"

"It means that you're fabricating stuff in your head for no reason."

"Well, it used to be that you wanted me every night, but now all of a sudden you don't. And I've been doing everything you said you wanted me to do."

But not the right way, Curtis thought. But that was beside the point, because regardless of how well she tried to make love to him now, she'd never be able to compare to Adrienne in a million years. She'd never be able to give him what Adrienne gave so naturally. Adrienne had always satisfied him without having to work at it, and he liked that. The chemistry they'd shared was unexplainable. It was the reason he was going to call her as soon as he hung up with Mariah.

"This is all in your head," he continued. "You're my wife, I love you, and I certainly don't want anyone else, if that's what you're thinking."

"Well, after finding out about that girl Charlotte, I don't know what to think."

"How many more times do I have to apologize for that?"

"You don't. But I just don't understand why our marriage seems to be changing."

"Look. I really don't have any more time for this, so unless you have something else to discuss, I need to prepare for my meeting. And you need to find something to do on your own."

"Honey, why are you treating me like this?" she said, starting to cry.

"Treating you like what, damn it?"

He regretted his words immediately. He hated using vulgarity, especially in the Lord's house, but Mariah was truly getting under his skin.

"I didn't mean to curse at you, and I'm sorry. But, baby, I really have to go."

"Fine."

"We'll talk more when I get home."

"How long do you think you'll be at the Wilsons'?"

"I don't know, but I'll call you when I leave there."

"I'll be waiting," she said.

"I love you, and I'll see you then."

"I love you, too."

Curtis felt like screaming. He'd wanted a wife who knew her place and one who would love him exclusively, but this was ridiculous. She was smothering him in a way he couldn't handle. He didn't want to lose her right now, because he needed a proper first lady, but she was going to have to stop expecting him to spend all of his free time with her. He'd never been confined in that way before and he wasn't going to allow it now. What he needed to do was have a long talk with her, so she understood how their marriage was going to work. But he would also make love to her at least every couple of days to prevent any further suspicions.

However, tonight wouldn't be one of those nights. He wasn't sure how his evening was going to play out, but earlier he'd sent Adrienne two dozen roses and called to see if she received them, and he was just about to call her again. She'd sounded sort of irritated and hadn't been able to talk for more than thirty seconds, but maybe if he prayed about it and spoke to her in just the right way, she'd finally agree to see him again. Hopefully, it would be tonight, since his schedule was wide open. It was true that he'd been asked to go visit the Wilsons, but he'd quickly fixed that situation as soon as the call came through. He had ten associate ministers and had already assigned one of them to do the honors. His associates were like faithful deputies and they stood in for him on a great number of occasions. Some of the deacons and quite a few of his members thought he should personally visit every family who'd lost a loved one, but he'd made it very clear that he wasn't going to do it. At least not all the time. Yes, he had done it quite often when he pastored at Faith, but when he'd signed on at Truth, he'd told the deacons that it was up to them and his associate ministers to handle those responsibilities. And the only reason he'd remotely considered visiting the Wilsons was that their son had recently signed a lucrative sports contract and had already mailed ten percent of his signing bonus to the church. But right now Adrienne was his priority and the Wilsons would just have to understand.

He picked up the sleek-looking silver cordless phone and then laid it back on its base. When he'd invited Adrienne to dinner a week ago and then called her this morning about the flowers, he'd made both calls from his office phone. But he was starting to think it might be better to use his cellular phone from here on out. He wasn't worried about anyone monitoring his phone calls, but after the way Monique, his former secretary at Faith, had spied on and betrayed him, he didn't want to take any chances. So instead he slid the earpiece into his ear, dialed Adrienne's office, and folded his arms across his stomach.

"So how are you?" he said when she answered.

She sighed but didn't speak.

"So are you still enjoying the flowers?"

"No, Curtis, I'm not. And do you want to know why? Because every single person in my department has been raving over how beautiful they are and how nice it was for my *husband* to send them. So, no, I'm not enjoying them one bit."

"I guess I don't know what to say."

"How about nothing?"

"Baby, look. I didn't mean to upset you, and I only sent them because I wanted you to know how much I've been thinking about you. I haven't been able to do much else since we had dinner."

"Well, I'd appreciate it if you wouldn't send me anything else."

"Okay. If that's how you feel, then I won't."

"Good. And if that's all, I have to go."

"Just like that?"

"What else do you expect me to do?"

"Talk to me."

"Look, Curtis. I don't know if you haven't been listening to me or if it's that you're just plain desperate when it comes to women. But either way, I want you to hear me once and for all: Please leave me the hell alone."

Desperate? Was she kidding? Yes, he wanted her back, but he certainly wasn't desperate, not by a long shot. He could have just about any woman he wanted. Inside the church or outside of it, for that matter. He wondered where she'd gotten such a lame idea and where all this sudden courage was coming from.

Five years ago she'd thought the sun rose and set on him, and she sometimes broke into tears just because he was angry at her.

But he knew this new attitude had everything to do with the fact that he'd been begging her like a sweet little puppy. He'd decided that the nice and polite route was the best way to go, but now he could see that it wasn't working. He also knew that deep down she wanted him back and was only trying to play hard to get. He'd seen it in her eyes when he'd kissed her in the parking ramp.

He knew what he had to do, though. He had to drop this nice-guy act and remind her of who she was dealing with.

"You know, Adrienne, I've poured my heart out to you, I've apologized, and still you're acting as if you hate my guts. As a matter of fact, I've been more patient with you than I have with any woman, but this is where it ends. And just for the record, I think you and I both know that I'm not anywhere near *desperate* when it comes to females."

"I have to go, Curtis."

"Fine. But just let me say one last thing. For the life of me, I can't believe you just ruined a chance at marrying a man who loves you as much as I do and who can give you everything you ever wanted. Not to mention the fact that you've blown a chance at being the next first lady at Truth. And this is all so you can stay married to that boring husband of yours—a man who probably couldn't satisfy a virgin when it comes to making love."

He waited for Adrienne to respond.

But she didn't.

"What a waste," Curtis said, and pressed the end button on his cell phone.

He'd finally rolled the dice and the only thing he could do now was wait for the outcome. There was no sure way to tell how Adrienne was going to react, but he was betting that she'd realize what a fool she'd been and would quickly come to her senses. He was counting on the fact that she'd soon realize she couldn't go on without him.

Curtis walked into the conference room and sat down at the highly shined mahogany table. The deacons and trustees filed in one and two at a time over the next ten minutes until they were all in attendance. They picked up meeting agendas from the table prior to sitting down.

"Before we call this meeting to order, let's first have a word of prayer," Deacon Gulley said. He was a husky middle-aged man, a former deacon at Faith and chairman of the board.

When he finished praying, he said, "Pastor Black has some new business to discuss, so I think we should start with that. Pastor?"

"Thank you, Deacon," Curtis said, leaning forward and resting his arms on the table. "As all of you know, I'm a pastor who believes in keeping up with the times and one who believes that even though this is a church, it has to be run in a businesslike manner. But before I get to what I'm proposing, let me tell you what's been happening the last four weeks. I asked six of my associate ministers to monitor the congregation to see if there was anything we could do to make things more convenient. And what they noticed was that there were a few cash-paying members who had fifty- and hundred-dollar bills but weren't able to get change for them. Which meant they couldn't pay their tithes and offerings. In addition to that, we've been receiving back far too many bad checks from the bank. So what I'm proposing is that we lease and install one or two ATMs in the front vestibule. That way, every member will have access to it, and it will even come in handy when we have unannounced offerings that they didn't bring enough cash for——"

"ATM?" Deacon Thurgood interrupted. "I know you don't

mean one of those money machines that I see at the grocery store and in certain parking lots?"

"Yes, Deacon, those are the machines I'm speaking about."

Deacon Thurgood looked at Deacon Winslow and shook his head in amazement. As Whitney had predicted, both men clearly disagreed with what Curtis was saying. But even though they were his elders and well into their seventies, he wasn't about to let them intimidate him.

"The other item I'm proposing is that we set up an electronic pay plan for members who pay the same tithe amount every pay period. That way, they'd be able to pay their tithes automatically. The benefit would be that they'd no longer have to write a check, carry cash, and when they aren't able to attend service for whatever reason, their tithes will still be deposited on a regular basis. This could also work for people who don't tithe but do give the same amount in offerings every Sunday. Then my final proposal is that we hire two financial planners who would meet with every member who isn't tithing. Some members don't tithe because they simply refuse to do what God has told them. Others can't afford it. But the reason they can't afford it is that they're not managing their money well enough. However, if we hire two qualified professionals, they could help members create budgets that will allow them to pay their ten percent and they'd also be able to pay off unnecessary debt and have more disposable income for themselves."

"I ain't never heard so much foolishness in all my life," Deacon Thurgood chimed in.

"Me neither, Fred," Deacon Winslow agreed. "And all these new ideas is what's sendin' folks straight to hell."

"You got that right, JC," Deacon Thurgood said. "Because that ATM and electronic payment stuff don't sound like nothin' but a scam to me."

Curtis prayed for someone else to comment. Anyone. But

everyone kept their mouths shut. Half the board members were in their thirties, so he couldn't understand why none of them had the balls to speak up. Spineless is what they were. But he wasn't going to show his frustration or anger and instead was going to talk this over with them "nicely."

"Okay, Deacons. I respect both of your opinions, but I'd also like to hear from the rest of the board. And let me just say right now that I'm not trying to propose any schemes here and that all moneys collected will still be deposited directly into the church account the same as always. I'm only proposing these ideas as a way to make giving more convenient for the members. And let's be honest, we can't run this church without the support of our tithes and offerings, so this will ultimately benefit the church as a whole."

"Well, I will say this," Deacon Taylor finally said. He was Curtis's favorite deacon and friend. "An ATM would definitely be convenient for me, because I'm always short on cash and then don't think about it until I really need it. And there probably are some members who just might appreciate having access to one inside the church. Especially on those days when they just don't have quite enough time to stop at another location."

"Well, I guess the next thang we'll be doin' is tellin' people they can pay by Visa, MasterCard, or Discover," Deacon Thurgood said.

"Mmm-mmm-mmm," Deacon Winslow said, laughing. "Paying the Lord with a credit card. Now ain't that a notion."

Deacon Thurgood joined him. "Ain't that somethin'? So, unh-unh, there ain't no way I can 'gree to nothin' like that."

"Naw, me neither, Fred."

Curtis wondered if Deacon Winslow always agreed with everything that *Fred* had to say. These two were running the entire meeting and he wondered when Deacon Gulley, the so-called chairman, was going to speak up.

"Mr. Chairman, how do you feel about my ideas?" Curtis asked.

"To be honest, Reverend, I really don't know. I do hear what you're saying, but I don't think the congregation is ready for ATMs and direct deposit. Or even financial planners for that matter. I know there are a few other churches out there that are already doing some of the things you're talking about, but I think we have to take things slow with our congregation. Because the one thing we don't want is for people to feel pressured into giving or like the ATM is an electronic guilt trip."

"I don't think they'd see it like that at all," Curtis said.

"It's really hard to say whether they would or wouldn't, but that's just how I feel," Deacon Gulley said.

"Well, what about everyone else? Deacon Jamison, Deacon Pryor, Deacon Evans?" Curtis polled the three youngest deacons in the room.

"I think you have some pretty good ideas, Pastor, but I just don't know if they're appropriate for this church," Deacon Evans stated.

"I second that. I don't totally disagree with what you want to do, but I'm not sure the timing is right," Deacon Jamison answered.

"And for me," Deacon Pryor said, "well, I guess, I'm just old-fashioned, so I don't see anything wrong with leaving our system of giving the way it is."

Cowards. Pure, unadulterated cowards. And what could Deacon Pryor possibly know about being old-fashioned? He couldn't have been more than thirty-three. Curtis didn't even want to think about the rest of the members sitting in the room and what they thought, let alone the ones who weren't able to attend the meeting. He was starting to feel like this was Faith Missionary all over again. Back then, the opposing ring leader was Deacon Jackson, but now he had Andy Taylor and Barney

Fife to contend with. He wanted to tell all of them how backwoods their way of thinking was and how they were never going to get anywhere by being so complacent. Didn't they know that change should be seen as something positive? Or that taking risks was very necessary in order to succeed?

"Well, if that's all you have, Pastor, then I think we should move on to the next order of business," Deacon Gulley suggested.

Curtis felt like a defeated heavyweight champion. He'd had so much more control and influence at Faith, but these deacons here at Truth seemed to be a little more on the stubborn side. He wasn't giving up, though. It was just going to take a little longer than he'd thought in terms of making them see the light.

And he had all the time in the world to wait.

Chapter 6

Mariah sliced two pieces of German chocolate cake, slid them on two separate plates, and walked back into the family room. She'd invited her mother over for a visit shortly after Curtis informed her that he wouldn't be home for dinner.

"Baby girl, this cake is too good," Jean told her.

"Isn't it, though. And it's not even homemade."

"Stop it. Are you serious?"

"Yes. I get it from the bakery down the street, and pretty much everything they make tastes wonderful."

"Well, it's a good thing my big ole self don't live anywhere near it, because I'd gain at least a pound or two every single day if I did," Jean said, chuckling.

"Mama, please. You're not nearly as heavy as you claim to be."

"Oh yes I am. Two hundred thirty pounds and only five six? That's way too heavy for any woman. But that's okay, because I'm about to try me another fad diet in a minute."

"When exactly is a minute, Mother?" Mariah asked.

"Just as soon as Easter, Memorial Day, and the Fourth of July are over with."

They both laughed.

"You are too, too much," Mariah added.

"I know. But tell me this. How is that fine-ass husband of yours doing?"

"I can't believe you."

"Girl, you know your mama calls everything the way she sees it. So it's not my fault that Curtis has that beautiful smooth chocolate skin and a body that screams sex every time I see him."

"Mama, you know you're embarrassing me."

"I don't know why. He's your husband and you should be proud of it. You did well for yourself, young lady, and your mama couldn't be more happy for you." Jean scanned the elegant cherry-wood china cabinet and eight-seat dining room table.

"Yeah, I guess I'm pretty happy, or at least I thought I was," Mariah said.

"Now what is that supposed to mean?" Jean set down her empty plate.

"I don't know, Mama. He's just not being as attentive as he was in the beginning, and he's always coming home well after dinner."

"Now, Mariah, you know that man is a big-time preacher with a lot of responsibilities, so you can't expect him to be at home with you all the time. If he was, you wouldn't have this house and everything in it."

"Maybe, but still something isn't right with us. And sometimes he speaks to me so harshly."

"Well, baby girl, I hope you're not nagging that man to death when you know all the pressure he must be under, trying to run that church."

"I don't nag him, Mama. I just want him to spend more time with me. And actually he was until maybe a couple of weeks ago."

"What you need to do is get out of this house more often. You were never a housewife before you married Curtis, so why are you hanging around here now waiting for him to get home? Because I'm telling you, baby girl, you're going to push him away if you keep doing all that complaining."

"What? Are you saying that I should go back to work?"

"No, I'm not saying that at all. I'm just saying you need to find some other interests. Get yourself a hobby of some kind or join some women's organization. You like helping people, so you could even volunteer for some charities. Anything that would get you out of here a few hours a day."

"I head up a young women's organization one day a week at the church, and I also teach a women's Bible study group every other Saturday morning."

"That's all fine and whatnot, but I'm talking about doing something outside of the church. You need to do something that's just for you and you only. Because even though you know I believe a man should take care of a woman, I also think she should have her own identity and do some things on her own."

"I guess."

"You've got yourself a real good man, but you've got to let him have a certain amount of freedom. You can't start making him feel all caught up. If you do, you'll end up forcing him into another woman's bed."

"But Curtis isn't perfect, Mama."

"Well, nobody is, baby girl. You know that."

"No, I mean, Curtis has some serious issues from his past that I just found out about."

"Like what?"

"Like an illegitimate five-year-old son that he never told me about. And the worst part of all is that the mother was only seventeen when he first started sleeping with her and this was all while he was married to his first wife."

"I know that probably hurt you, Mariah, but the past is exactly that. Everybody makes mistakes, but people do change."

"Well then, why didn't he tell me on his own instead of letting me find out from someone else?"

"Who told you?"

"Nobody really. I heard Alicia say it when she was yelling and screaming at him about how he'd ruined their family."

"I know this is a little off the subject, but is she starting to warm up to you any?" Jean asked.

"No, and now she's totally disrespecting Curtis, too."

"She's just hurt because her parents aren't together anymore. And as wonderful as you are to her, she sees you as someone who's in her way."

"I know, but I wish she would just realize that I only want to love her like my own child."

"She will eventually. You'll see."

"I'm just starting to wonder what I got myself into when I married Curtis. Sometimes I think we can pray for the wrong things."

"Now look. I don't ever want to hear you talk like that again. Because I know you haven't forgotten that run-down, roach-infested shack we used to live in. It saddens me every time I think about it, but what makes me so happy now is that one of my babies got an education, married a wealthy man, and made it all the way to the top. Both your sisters are almost forty and still living at home with me, one of your brothers is serving a life sentence for being a drug dealer, one is barely two steps from joining him, and the other is living with a woman and using her. So I'm telling you, baby girl, you might be the youngest, but of all my children, you have the best head on your shoulders and the biggest heart. I know I may not have been the best mother in the world, but I loved you and tried to take care of you the best I could. So that's why I don't want to see

you give up what you have. I don't want you to be unhappy, and
I don't ever wanna see any man walking all over you, but please
try to make your marriage work if you can."

"I am trying, but Curtis has to meet me halfway."

"I'm sure everything will be fine," Jean said, reaching out for
her daughter. "And no matter what, I'll always be here for you."

Mariah hugged her mother and wished she never had to let
her go.

"I know that, Mama, and I love you so much."

"I love you, too, baby girl. And don't you ever forget that. Not
for as long as you live."

At that moment Mariah realized how strong a mother's love
could be and decided that maybe it was time she became one
herself. Yes, Curtis had said he wanted to wait, but starting a
family would bring them so much closer. And she wouldn't
have to spend so much time alone when he had business to attend to. She'd finally have another human being that she could
love unconditionally and spend all of her time with. She'd have
a baby that would love and appreciate her until the end.

She'd finally have everything.

Curtis drove into the subdivision and saw his mother-in-law's
car parked in his driveway. But just as he did, his phone rang.
He figured it was Mariah, until he saw the word "unknown"
displayed on the screen.

"Hello?"

"All I can say is that I must be completely insane to be calling you back," Adrienne said. "And I know that I'm going to regret this for the rest of my life."

"Is that so?" Curtis said rather coolly, and pulled his car to
the side of the street. He wanted Adrienne to think he was still
angry about their earlier conversation.

"Yes. But while I hate admitting it, you were right about

everything you said. I am still in love with you, and I'm completely miserable with Thomas. He'd make the perfect husband for someone else, but he's just not for me. I've really tried to be happy with him, but it's just not working."

"I've told you before that not every married couple is compatible or meant to be together. And no matter how hard you try to make it work, it won't get any better. Because even though I've tried to be happy with Mariah, she's just not enough for me. She's not the woman I'm supposed to be married to, and it's like I told you before, she's not you."

There was a pause and then Curtis heard Adrienne sniffle.

"Baby, what are you crying about?"

"The fact that I'm so confused and I'm so afraid that if we start seeing each other again, it's going to end up a total disaster. I'm scared to death that things will turn out worse than they did five years ago."

"But I promise you they won't. This isn't like before, and as soon as I divorce Mariah, you and I can finally be married."

"I want to believe you, Curtis. I really do. But you know that's hard for me after all that has happened."

"I understand that, but if you just give me this one last chance, I'll prove everything to you."

"But what if Thomas finds out? Or Mariah for that matter?"

"Nobody's going to find out anything. We'll be even more careful than we were in the past, and it will only be for a short time."

"I just don't know."

"Why don't we talk about this face-to-face," he said, rolling the dice again.

"When?"

"Tonight?"

"I don't know. It's already after eight."

"Where are you now?"

"Still at my office."

"Why don't we get together for maybe an hour or so?"

"But Thomas knows that even when I work late, I'm usually home by eight-thirty."

"Tell him you're going out with some coworkers. Tell him anything, because, baby, I really need to see you."

"Curtis, what are we doing?"

"We're about to stop being miserable."

"Where do you want to meet?" she said.

"The usual place?"

"Fine. I'll see you in about forty-five minutes."

"See you then."

Curtis gazed at his house again, did a U-turn in the middle of the street, and drove back out of the subdivision. To his surprise, he felt a tad bit guilty and somewhat sorry for Mariah. He'd honestly tried to be faithful to her. He'd tried to do what he knew God wanted him to, but it wasn't his fault that Mariah couldn't satisfy him or make him happy. In actuality, it wasn't her fault either, because she couldn't help being the person she was.

He picked up speed after entering the interstate and said out loud, "Lord forgive me for what I'm about to do."

When they arrived at the hotel, Adrienne went in, checked into a room, phoned Curtis on his cell phone, and gave him the room number. They'd agreed that it was best to walk in separately just in case they saw someone they knew. Curtis had been somewhat nervous when they'd gone to the restaurant last week, but he'd decided it was well worth the risk. Rarely had they eaten together out in the open during their first affair, so he figured taking her to a public establishment would be impressive. And impressive it was, because he was sure it had helped convince her that she needed him more than ever.

Curtis took the elevator up to the eighth floor and walked

down the corridor to 803. Adrienne opened the door, and he grabbed her in his arms instantly. They kissed madly and Curtis unzipped the fitted gray dress she was wearing. He slid it off each shoulder and pushed it down toward the floor. She stepped out of it, and Curtis unsnapped her bra and laid her on the bed. They kissed again and he removed everything else she was wearing. Then he removed his own blazer, all the while admiring her body and shaking his head in amazement. She hadn't aged one day, and her body was still just as beautiful as he remembered.

He loosened his tie and began shedding the rest of his clothing. He continued staring at her, barely able to contain himself, and Adrienne lay there watching him with tears streaming down her face. They hadn't said one word to each other, and they both agreed silently that there were no more words to speak. At least not now, anyway, because they'd come here solely to express their feelings and desire for each other.

Curtis made love to her like he never had before. He moved his tongue between her legs like an artist twirling a paintbrush. She moaned and groaned and wept, and Curtis turned up the intensity a whole other notch. He could tell he was driving her wild, and loved all the juice her body was producing. He buried his head deeper and deeper until she screamed at the top of her lungs.

He lifted his body away from her and she sat up and reached her hand toward his crotch. She pulled him into her mouth and Curtis thought he had died and gone to heaven.

"Oh dear God," he declared, closing his eyes. "That's what I'm talking about."

Adrienne was still a master when it came to oral sex, and now he knew he had to say and do whatever it took to keep her in his life.

She moved her lips upward and downward, slowly and then more rapidly, tightening her grasp.

Curtis felt himself preparing to come and pulled away from her.

Then he laid her down and slid inside her.

"Baby, I want you to promise me that you won't ever give yourself to another man for as long as you live," he said.

Adrienne groaned with much satisfaction as he eased in and out of her.

"Baby, did you hear me?" Curtis asked, entering her a bit harder than before.

"Yes, Curtis, I heard you."

"Then tell me that you're all mine, and that you will never give yourself to another man from this day forward. Not even the deacon."

"Curtis, please."

"No," he said, pulling out of her and then in with more force. "I want you to promise me."

"Okay, Curtis. I promise. I'm all yours."

"I mean it, baby," he said. "I wouldn't be able to stand it if you gave this to someone else."

"I promise, baby. I won't."

"Not even the deacon," he said, increasing his speed, and then suddenly he pulled out of her again.

"Curtis, please don't keep torturing me like this. Please just give it to me."

"Not even the deacon," he repeated.

In. And out.

"No, Curtis. I won't even give it to him."

"You know I love you, don't you?"

In. And out.

"Yes. And I love you. I've always loved you."

"And you'd do anything for me, wouldn't you?" he said, forcing her knees toward her chest, pushing himself in and out of her, repeatedly, with all the power and strength he could muster. She moaned repeatedly, and Curtis continued in a lyrical yet forceful rhythm until his body exploded.

They held each other, savoring the excitement. At least that's how Curtis was feeling, anyway, and he hoped Adrienne was satisfied. He wasn't sure what had come over him, but all he knew was that he'd never made love so aggressively until tonight. In a matter of minutes he'd felt this great need to be in control and, as much as he hated to admit it, like he needed Adrienne to know who was in charge. Like he needed to fulfill some burning desire he'd never had before.

"You must have really missed me," she said.

"That's an understatement, but why do you ask?"

"Because I've never seen you act this way before. It was almost like you hadn't had sex in years."

"To be honest, it feels like I haven't. No one has ever come close to giving me the pleasure you do. And Mariah has got to be the worst I've ever had."

"Yeah, right," she said, catching her breath.

"I'm serious. With her, it's missionary style all the way, and you know that bores the crap out of me."

"Well, I hope you just released every one of those pent-up desires, because you were a little rough toward the end."

"I didn't hurt you, did I?" He turned toward her, genuinely concerned.

"No, but it was different and you sort of caught me off guard."

"I'll try not to do that again, because I don't ever want to hurt you," he said, kissing her forehead.

They lay speechless again with Curtis stroking Adrienne's hair.

"Thank you," he said.

"For what?"

"For meeting me at the restaurant the other night and for allowing me a chance to make things right with you."

"That's fine and well, but as soon as we walk out of here, it's back to reality. I have to go home to Thomas and you have to go home to Mariah."

"But this isn't about them. This is about us. And I was serious when I said I don't want you having sex with the deacon anymore."

"And what about you and Mariah?" she asked. "Are you prepared to stop having sex with her, too?"

Curtis was somewhat surprised, because in the old days he'd made all sorts of demands but Adrienne never questioned him about anything. She never had the nerve. But now she was definitely a woman with a new attitude. She was definitely someone he was going to have to handle very carefully now that they were seeing each other again. He'd *try* to be faithful to her for as long as he could, but that's all he could promise. And he wouldn't even tell her that out loud because he knew what he was capable of.

"I won't sleep with Mariah either," he agreed.

"Curtis, I ask you again, what are we doing? What am I doing to myself?"

"You're spending time with the man you love, I'm spending time with the woman I love, and that's all that matters."

"I hate this. I hate that we're about to start all this sneaking around again. I almost lost everything last time, so you have to be very sure about this. You have to be positive that you're going to divorce Mariah in six months, and that I'm going to be your wife."

"Baby, all you have to do is trust me, because I'm really serious this time. I'm really going to marry you," he said, and wondered what lie he'd have to come up with once the six-month deadline began approaching. He wished there was a way he could marry Adrienne, because if he were ever going to love any woman exclusively, it would have been her. But there was no way he could leave Mariah. She was perfect. She was naïve, and she obeyed him. What more could a man ask for? What more could a pastor of a prominent church want? If he married Adrienne, she'd end up being the same as Tanya, ranting and raving about everything he did and then whining about all the hours he spent away from home. He couldn't be harassed like that ever again, so Adrienne would just have to understand. He wasn't sure how, but he had to make her see that the two of them weren't marriage material, and that a lifetime affair was so much more becoming. It was so much more interesting.

He had to make her see that his love for her was sincere, and that if she stayed with him, he would take care of all her financial and emotional needs forever. She'd have the best of everything. She would never want for anything.

He had to make her see that she was being offered a much better way of life than she was currently living. A much happier life than she had with the deacon.

Chapter 7

Alicia pressed the entry code on the keypad near the garage and waited for it to open. It was Friday, so right after school she'd gone shopping with Danielle and her mother and was just now arriving home.

Once inside the house, she strolled toward the kitchen and saw her mother and James standing at the island. They looked as if the world had come to an end. Now what?

"What's wrong?" she asked them.

"Apparently a whole lot," Tanya answered. "Because only minutes ago, your counselor just informed me that you've been skipping your math class all week."

Alicia gazed at them, but decided it was probably best not to respond. Especially since her mother looked like she wanted to kill her.

"So why haven't you been going?" Tanya asked.

"I don't know."

"You don't know? What do you mean you don't know?" Tanya asked with fire in her eyes, moving closer to Alicia. "Last week we found out you were failing world history, now this."

"Sweetheart," James said to Tanya. "Why don't we all go

into the family room so we can sit down and discuss this more calmly."

"No, what I want is for Miss Alicia to explain herself right here and right now."

Alicia's stomach churned, but she was also starting to despise her mother's crazy attitude.

"Girl, don't you hear me talking to you?" Tanya continued.

"Yes."

"Then why aren't you answering my question?"

"Because, Mom. I don't know why I skipped math."

"James, are you listening to this?" Tanya said.

James raised his eyebrows in silence. He'd learned early on that it was better not to interfere in his wife and stepdaughter's confrontations.

"Alicia, I'm really to the point where I don't know what to do with you," Tanya continued. "And I'm completely fed up with all of these reports we keep getting from your school."

"Maybe I should just go live with Daddy," Alicia threatened.

"You know, Alicia, maybe you should. Maybe it's time that you moved out of here and in with your father and Mariah. Maybe I've done all I can do."

Alicia was stunned. Usually her mother became highly upset whenever she spoke about going to live with her father, so she hadn't expected this response at all. She didn't know what to say next, but the one thing she did know was that she'd rather die than go live with her father and his wife.

"What do you think, James?" Tanya asked. "Because maybe it really is time Alicia went to live with Curtis. Maybe he can get her to go to class and do her schoolwork the way she's supposed to."

"Sweetheart," James said. "I don't think that's necessarily the solution."

"Well, is this what you really want to do, Alicia?" Tanya asked.

"I don't know."

Tanya laughed sarcastically. "Well, is there anything that you *do* know?"

"Yes," Alicia spoke boldly, yet in tears. "I know that you and Daddy are divorced and that we're never going to be a family again."

"Alicia, I realize you've had a tough time with all of this, and yes, you're right. Things are never going to be the way they once were. I wish, for your sake, that they could be, but they can't. I know you're still feeling a tremendous amount of pain, but I just don't know how to help you anymore. When we were in counseling a couple of years ago, you seemed to come to terms with everything, so why is this all of a sudden becoming a major issue again? You seemed fine until a few months ago."

Alicia wanted to tell her how right she was. Because until her father married Mariah, she'd still held on to the possibility of her mother and him getting back together. She'd known her mother was married to James, but as long as her father was still available, she'd kept high hopes. She'd even prayed about it every chance she got. She'd even figured out a way for it to happen where no one would get hurt. James would accidentally meet another woman, fall in love, and then tell her mother that he couldn't be with her any longer. But her mother would be fine with it because deep down she'd really want to be back with Alicia's father, anyway. Alicia had played that scene in her head at least a thousand times, but the curtain had been yanked shut the day her father married Mariah. That stupid fairy-tale wedding of theirs had ruined everything.

"Pumpkin, do you think it would help for you to go to counseling again?" James asked Alicia.

"I don't know . . . I mean, maybe."

"Why don't we do that then?" James said, turning his attention to Tanya.

"That's fine," Tanya said. "Because I'm willing to do whatever it takes."

"Can I be excused?" Alicia asked.

"Yes, but until you get your grades back up to where they should be, you won't be going anywhere except school, church, and back home."

"But, Mom, I have Camille's birthday party this weekend."

"Not anymore you don't. Because starting today, you're grounded until further notice."

"Why are you doing this?" Alicia said, sobbing. "Why are you and Daddy always trying to make my life so miserable?"

"Look, Alicia. I've said what I have to say, and I don't want to hear any more back talk from you."

Alicia left the kitchen and went fuming up to her bedroom. She hated her mother almost as much as she hated her father. As a matter of fact, James was the only adult in her life who had any sense. He never harassed her about silly stuff, he never yelled at her, and he always went out of his way to do nice things for her. She was starting to wish that he was her biological father, and that she had a different mother to go along with him. And she was never going to forgive her mother for making her miss Camille's birthday bash. Camille's parents owned a top black magazine and were filthy rich. They were even sending a limo to pick up Camille's closest friends. Not to mention the actual party they were having downtown at the Four Seasons. They were expecting two hundred guests and had rented a suite for Camille and five of her friends. Alicia, of course, was one of them. Her mother had said that it was ridiculous for any parent to spend thousands on any child who was just turning fifteen, but what did she know? Maybe Camille's parents were doing it because *they* truly loved their daughter. Maybe they actually knew how to treat a child that they'd voluntarily brought into this world.

Alicia lay across her bed, still weeping. When she finally calmed herself, she glanced over at her computer. Julian always made her feel better and she was starting to realize that he was the only person she could turn to. Yes, she had her best friend, Danielle, but it wasn't the same as when she shared her feelings with Julian. As a matter of fact, she hadn't even told Danielle about her chats with him, because she wasn't sure how Danielle would take it. Sometimes she blew the tiniest things out of proportion, so Alicia had decided not to mention her new on-line buddy. At least not yet, anyway.

She kicked off her tan platform shoes that mimicked those designed in the seventies and sat down at her desk. Usually when her mother said she was grounded, that also included telephone and Internet privileges, but what her mother didn't know wouldn't hurt her.

She signed on to AOL and waited. As soon as she heard the words "You've Got Mail," she turned down the volume on her computer. She would keep it at mute status until she was no longer on punishment.

She checked her e-mail messages and broke into tears again when she read the one from Camille. It was a note informing everyone that her parents had called in a favor and now a surprise hip-hop music artist was going to be singing at her birthday party. If it was someone Alicia was a big fan of, she would never speak to her mother again.

She read a message from Danielle about homework, and smiled when she saw that Julian had just signed on to his account. She quickly sent him an instant message.

ALICIABLK: Hey, Julian.
JMONEY1: Alicia! What's up with you this evening?
ALICIABLK: You don't even want to know. ☹
JMONEY1: Hey, now what's with the sad face?

ALICIABLK: My mother is acting just as crazy as my father
    was last week.
JMONEY1: I'm sorry to hear that. You've really been having
    it out with your parents a lot lately, haven't you?
ALICIABLK: Yes, and I'm really getting sick of it. Sometimes
    I feel like I don't have anyone, and if I didn't have you to
    talk to, I don't know what I would do.
JMONEY1: You know I'm always here for you. I just wish I
    could talk to you by phone or see you in person.

And why couldn't they speak by phone? Every time he mentioned talking to her or getting together, she sort of shied away
from it, but maybe if she could hear his voice, she'd actually
feel better.

ALICIABLK: What's your phone number?
JMONEY1: (312) 555-2823.
ALICIABLK: Do you want me to call right now?
JMONEY1: I've got the phone sitting right here. So all you
    have to do is dial the number. ☺
ALICIABLK: Okay.

Alicia lifted the receiver and thanked God she'd convinced
her mother to install a separate phone line for her. The only ex-
tension was in her bedroom, so at least there was no way her
mother could eavesdrop or suddenly pick up the phone, yelling
at her to get off it. The worst that could happen was her storm-
ing into the bedroom, but she still wouldn't be able to find out
who Alicia was talking to. And if that happened, Alicia would
lie and say it was Danielle, because she and Danielle main-
tained a permanent pact. They'd promised each other two years
ago that if one of their parents ever questioned them about
anything, they'd lie for each other until the end. To this day,

Danielle had never let her down. Although sometimes she tended to be a little fearful, and that was the real reason Alicia hadn't told her about Julian.

She dialed the number displayed on her monitor and waited for Julian to answer.

"So what's up?" he said.

"Not much." She was more nervous than she'd imagined, but she loved the sound of his voice. It was so deep, and he sounded so cool!

"You sound like you're uncomfortable with this."

"No . . . not really."

"I like your voice."

"I like yours, too."

"So. Tell me what's going on with your moms."

"I missed my math class a couple of times this week, and she went crazy."

"Well, you know how most parents are when it comes to the school thing."

"Was your mother like that when you were in school?"

"No, she couldn't have cared less whether I went or not. But my stepmoms made sure I got to school and did my homework. And for the most part, I didn't have to do a lot of studying. I used to study for tests the night before and still get an A on them," he said.

"I'm sort of like that, too, but lately I don't feel like doing any of my assignments. Sometimes I don't even bother to answer all the questions on my tests. It just depends on how I feel."

"Why is that?"

"Because I'm just not motivated and because me getting good grades is all they seem to care about."

"You do need good grades if you're planning to get a good job or go to college."

"You didn't go college, and you already have your own place."

"Yeah, but it's only because I have my own business, and I make a shitload of money doing what I do."

"I can't believe so many people buy CDs from you and that you have so many regular customers." Alicia was amazed.

"People love music, and that's one thing in this world that won't ever change."

"I guess not."

"So tell me. When am I going to get a chance to see you?"

Alicia was hoping he wouldn't bring this subject up so quickly. She was hoping the phone call would suffice for a while.

"I don't know," she said. "But soon."

"Soon was fine until I heard your voice. Because, girl, you sound so sweet, and now I can't wait to kick it with you. I can't wait to take you out to dinner or wherever you wanna go."

"I can't wait either," was all she could think to say.

"Well, can I ask you something else?"

"What?"

"Are you sexually active?"

"Why do you ask?"

"I'm just wondering, because your voice is so sexy, and you sound much older than seventeen. You sound more mature than some twenty-year-old women I know."

"Yeah, right," Alicia said, beaming.

"I'm serious. You do."

"Whatever, Julian."

"And to tell you the truth, I'm starting to wish you hadn't called me."

"Why?"

"Because hearing your voice is bringing out some feelings I didn't know I had. Especially for a woman I haven't even seen before."

"What kind of feelings?" She was a little bit confused by what he was saying and needed him to explain. But she loved that he saw her as a woman and not some childish little girl.

"I'd better not say."

"Why?"

"I don't want to embarrass myself," he said, laughing.

"Come on, Julian. Tell me."

"Girl, don't start somethin' you won't be able to finish."

"Like what?"

"Okay, look. I don't usually fall for women just from chatting with them on-line or by talking to them on the phone, but, girl, you're makin' me crazy."

"Are you saying you like me like a girlfriend?"

"That's exactly what I'm saying."

Alicia was afraid to ask any further questions, because she didn't know where the rest of the conversation was headed. But the truth of the matter was she could tell she had feelings for him, too. She had to remind herself that Julian wasn't one of those little boys at her school and that she had to act as grown as she knew how to.

"But we haven't even seen each other before," she said.

"I know, but I'm tellin' you, girl, I've got some straight-up real feelings for you, and if I knew you better, I'd show you just how serious they are, right here on the phone. I'd make you feel the way every woman is supposed to feel."

"And how would you do that?"

"You don't even want to know."

"Yes I do," she said, and wondered how in the world he could show her anything through the phone. He was so silly.

"I know you've heard of phone sex, haven't you?"

"Yeah . . . I guess so."

"Well?"

"I don't know, Julian."

"Why? Are you afraid?"

"No." She spoke quickly.

"Then why? It can't hurt anything and it's the safest sex you can have."

"What if my mother walks in and catches me on the phone with you?"

"If you think she might come into your room, then we won't do it."

"I just don't know, Julian, because I've never done anything like this before."

"All you have to do is listen."

"And then what?"

"You do the things I ask you to do. Okay?"

She was terrified that her mother might burst into her room at any moment, but a part of her wanted to hear what Julian had to say.

"Okay," she agreed.

"What do you have on?"

"A knit top with a chiffon blouse over it."

"Pants or a skirt?"

"Jeans."

"Well, I need you to take all of that off."

"Everything?"

"Yes."

Alicia hesitated, but then told him, "Hold on for a minute."

When she'd removed everything except her bra and panties, she picked up the phone.

"Okay, I did it," she said.

"You took off everything?"

"Yes."

"Even your underwear?"

"No . . . I mean, you didn't say that you wanted me to."

"Well, it's up to you, but this will work so much better if you take off everything."

Alicia removed her bra but simply couldn't will herself to remove her panties. That was going too far and she just didn't feel comfortable doing it.

"Okay, now what?" she asked.

"You took everything off, right?"

"Yes. Everything."

"Do you have a headset for your phone?"

"Yes." Although the only reason she had one was that she and Danielle loved talking to each other and surfing the Internet simultaneously for hours at a time. Sometimes they did research for papers they had to write and sometimes they did it just for fun.

Alicia put on the headset.

"You ready?"

"Yes."

"Okay, now close your eyes."

Alicia followed his instructions and waited nervously.

"Take both your hands and massage both your nipples until you feel them getting hard."

Alicia bugged her eyes open and covered her mouth with both hands.

"And I mean massage them until it feels so good that you don't ever want to stop."

Alicia didn't move.

"Are you doing it?" he asked.

"Yes," she said, and covered her mouth again.

"I bet it feels real good, doesn't it? And if I was there with you, I'd suck both those titties like a baby suckin' his bottle."

Alicia burst into laughter.

"What's so funny?"

He sounded irritated, and now she was sorry she'd laughed at him.

"Nothing," she finally answered. She was still sniggering.

"Well, somethin' must be real funny or you wouldn't be crackin' up like that."

"I'm sorry, Julian. I didn't mean to."

"No, I'm the one who's sorry, because I had no idea you were so immature. You sound a lot older than seventeen, but now I'm wondering if you're even in high school yet."

"I am seventeen," she insisted.

"Whatever. But hey, I'm gettin' ready to bounce, okay?"

"But, Julian?"

"But, Julian, what?"

"Please don't be mad at me."

"I'm not mad, just disappointed."

"I'm so sorry, and I promise I'll make this up to you."

"And how do you plan on doing that?"

"I don't know, but I will."

"Well, like I said, I have to go."

"Are you going to be on-line again tomorrow?"

"Maybe. Who knows?"

"You're really, really mad at me, aren't you?"

"I told you I wasn't. Now I have to go."

He hung up and Alicia felt so stupid. How could she have been so childish when all he'd done was try to make her feel like a woman? She had to make him realize how sorry she was and that she was more than willing to try that phone sex thing again. This time she would do everything he told her and she wouldn't do one thing to upset him.

She grabbed her bra, hooked it back on, and heard a knock at her door.

"Yes," Alicia said.

Her mother walked in. "What are you doing?"

"Nothing. I'm just changing out of my school clothes."

"Do you have homework?"

"Yes."

"Then as soon as you finish dinner, that's what I want you to work on for the rest of the evening. Oh, and by the way, being grounded also means no personal phone calls and no Internet."

"But, Mom—"

"I mean it, Alicia," Tanya said, and closed her daughter's door.

Alicia fell across her bed and wished she lived in another household.

Chapter 8

Mariah fastened the last button on the crème-colored silk blouse and tucked it inside her black linen skirt. Now she wished she'd bought the skirt in at least two other colors, because the wide waistband slimmed her down more than usual. She'd found it at Saks several months ago, and since she and her friend Vivian were planning to go shopping in a couple of days, it wouldn't hurt to see if they still had them.

She did a once-over in the mirror to confirm that her makeup was intact and to see if her hair was still in place. She glanced at her watch and saw that she had ninety minutes to get to the church. Every Wednesday she oversaw and advised a teenage group called YGM, an acronym for Young Girls Ministry. In any given week there were usually twenty to thirty attendees, and Mariah loved working with them. They came from all walks of life and not all of them were actual members of the church. Wanting to make a difference in the community, she'd started the ministry right after marrying Curtis. She'd told him that there were so many underprivileged children with problems in the city of Chicago, but that she wanted to concentrate on teenage girls, ages seventeen through nineteen.

Specifically those who came from broken homes, those who had already had a baby or had had an abortion, and those who had lost all interest in going to school. She was proud of what she was doing, because the ministry had only started out with five or six girls.

Mariah lifted her Louis Vuitton tote from the dresser, slid her Bible inside, and grabbed her car keys. After setting the alarm system, she left the house and drove out of the driveway. Even with traffic, she would arrive at the church almost an hour early, but that was how she'd planned it. The YGM gathering always ended about a half hour before weekly Bible study, and she could easily speak to Curtis in between, but she wanted to have a short talk with him beforehand. He hadn't come home until well after nine again last night, and she was really starting to get worried.

Last Monday it was the writing of his sermon that had kept him out late. Last Tuesday he'd had a meeting with the deacons and trustees and then had to go sit and pray with the Wilsons because of a death in their family. It seemed like there was one excuse right after another, and with the exception of four days ago, when he'd taken her to a Saturday matinee and then dinner on Sunday, she hadn't seen very much of him. Yes, he'd made love to her on each of those days, but he hadn't touched her on Monday or last night. She'd questioned him about his whereabouts, but when she'd noticed how irritated he was becoming, she'd stopped. She'd decided that it was best to sleep on everything she was thinking and then discuss it with him this morning. But by the time she woke up, he was already showered, dressed, and on his way out. She'd made another attempt at questioning him, but he insisted he had an early morning meeting, and that they would have to speak later.

She drove into the church parking lot, parked her car, and then headed straight up to Curtis's study.

"Hi, Whitney," Mariah said to Curtis's secretary.

"Hi, Sister Black. How are you?" She stood and hugged Mariah.

"I'm well."

"Same here. Are you here to see Pastor?"

"As a matter of fact I am. Is he in there?"

"Yes."

Mariah knocked once and entered Curtis's study.

"Do you have a few minutes?" she asked.

"What kind of question is that? Because you know I have all the time in the world for my beautiful wife."

He stood, walked toward her, and kissed her on the lips.

Mariah pushed his door shut and wondered why his tone was much more pleasant than it had been over the last couple of weeks. She wondered if he was just putting on airs for Whitney, wanting her to think their marriage was perfect.

"Well, Curtis, it really doesn't seem like that lately," she said, sitting down in front of him.

He leaned against his desk. "I know, baby, but it's truly been a very rough month for me. I'm preparing sermons every week, trying to get the officers to agree with some of the things I'm proposing, and you know all the other responsibilities I have with the members. I know I haven't been spending as much time with you, but, baby, duty calls."

"I understand all of that, but still something seems different. You're different."

"Different, how?"

"You're staying out much later than normal and you act like you don't even have the same desire for me."

"Only because I'm tired all the time. And it's not like I'm twenty years old anymore. I'm thirty-eight."

"You were also thirty-eight just a few weeks ago, but it didn't seem to be a problem."

"But I just told you, I've been very tired."

"I know that, but I'm still worried about our marriage."

"Well, I don't know what to tell you, baby, except that I love you and that you and Alicia are the two most important people in this world to me."

"But, Curtis, I'm sure she's feeling neglected, too, because you really don't spend much time with her either. And I'm sure she thinks I'm the reason you don't, and that's why she doesn't have much to say to me."

"Alicia knows that I love her and that being a pastor means I can't spend as much time with her as I'd like to. Even when I was pastor at Faith, she always understood that. She was only a little girl, but she even understood it better than her mother."

"Look, I know you have a lot of responsibilities here at the church, but I just didn't know it was going to take you away from me day and night. It wasn't like that in the beginning, so that's why I'm trying to figure out what's going on now."

"Look, I'm sorry that you're unhappy, but this is pretty much how it's going to be. I won't always be as busy as I was this past month, but being a pastor is a twenty-four-hour job. You never know what's going to happen or when you're going to be called."

"Then I guess I don't have a choice but to get used to it. Is that what you're saying?"

Curtis pulled Mariah up from the chair and held her hands. "It's not that you don't have a choice, baby, but I need you to stand by me. I need you to support what I'm trying to do as a minister. And more than anything, I need you to keep loving me."

"I do love you, Curtis. You know that. But I still feel like something is missing. I mean maybe it's time we started thinking about a baby. I know you said you wanted to wait awhile so we could have some time alone, but I think it's time for us to start right now."

"Yeah, but the thing is, you still really haven't bonded with Alicia, and now with the way she's acting, she'll really be upset if we brought a new baby into the picture."

"But how am I supposed to bond with her when she's only around every other weekend? And even then she doesn't say any more than what I ask her."

"I don't know. But I still think having a baby will push her away even further. So it's just not the right time," he said, walking away from her and back around his desk.

"Well, when will it be?"

"I don't know. Maybe next year. Maybe sooner."

"What difference is a few months going to make?"

He was really starting to anger her and she couldn't help wondering if Alicia was the real reason he wanted them to hold off on having a baby.

"A few months can make a world of difference when you're talking about the emotional well-being of a child. You know Alicia hasn't been herself, and now she's all of a sudden having problems at school. So the last thing I want is to make her even more rebellious."

"So that's your final decision? We have to wait until next year?"

"I'm sorry, but yes."

"Fine, Curtis."

Mariah grabbed her tote and turned toward the door. It was all she could do to keep from crying.

"Baby, wait," he said, walking toward her. "I know you're upset, but I really need you to understand why we have to take our time with this."

She turned and faced him, tears flowing down her cheeks. She couldn't remember the last time she'd felt so unhappy.

Curtis pulled her into his arms. "Baby, why are you crying? I mean, is having a baby right away that important to you?"

"Yes. It is."

Curtis sighed deeply. "Okay, I'll tell you what. Give me a few months to see if I can help Alicia with whatever it is she's going through, and then we'll start trying."

Mariah still didn't see why they had to wait. Especially since she knew he wasn't going to make any real attempt at rebuilding his relationship with Alicia. These days he seemed to have an excuse for everything, and Mariah wondered when the man she married was going to show up again. She wondered because this certainly wasn't the same man she'd fallen in love with and made a commitment to.

"Is that okay with you?" he asked. "Can you at least wait that long?"

"Fine. Whatever you want, Curtis."

"It's not just about me, because I want us both to agree on this."

"If we have to wait, then we have to wait."

"Thank you, baby, for being so understanding. And I promise you, it won't take as long as you think."

If that were true, then why was her intuition telling her something different?

Why was she feeling like things were only going to get worse between them?

"The only thing my mother ever cared about was smoking her crack pipe," Ebony said to Mariah and the other twenty YGM members in attendance. They were sitting in one of the classrooms located on the educational wing of the church and had been for thirty minutes.

"She never kept food in the house and she never did anything for me or my brother and sister," Ebony continued. "And because I'm the oldest, I had to make sure they had something to eat and clothes to put on their backs. I had to do whatever I could, and that's why I ended up dropping out of school."

"You shouldn't have had to take on your mother's responsibilities, but you will definitely be blessed for taking care of your siblings," Mariah said.

"But, see, that's what I don't understand, Sister Black. I don't understand why I had to be born into this situation to begin with. I mean, why couldn't I have had a mother like you or some other woman who cares about people? Why couldn't I have been given two parents who are married to each other and who are working hard to take care of their children?"

These were the types of questions that always bothered Mariah because there were never any real answers. It especially bothered her when the questions came from someone like Ebony, a highly intelligent eighteen-year-old who was currently enrolled in a GED program but clearly belonged at a top university. It was hard to explain that everything happened for a reason, and that joy really did come in the morning the way the Bible promised.

But Mariah tried to answer as best as she could. "I don't know why you ended up with the life you have or even why I grew up the way I did, but I do know that if you stay prayerful and keep your faith in God, everything will work out the way it's supposed to. I'm a living witness to all that I'm saying. I grew up on the West Side of Chicago with five brothers and sisters and we barely had food to eat. And it wasn't because my mother didn't care about us or because she did drugs. It was simply because she had six children and never got help from either of the two men she conceived us with. But she's the first one to admit that she never should have kept having children, knowing that the men in her life were no good and that she wasn't married to either of them. My life back then was hard, but it still didn't stop me from doing the best I could in school or from going to college. And even though we were poor, that ended up being a blessing, because that's how I qualified for all the financial aid I received. I majored in accounting and eventually became the director of grants and funding at the largest social service agency here in Chicago. And of course, that's where I met my husband."

"And now you're livin' as large as you wanna be," Rayshonna said. "And married to that fine ole Pastor Black."

All the girls laughed at Rayshonna. She was the comedian of the group and the liveliest.

"You're terrible," Mariah said teasingly.

"I'm just callin' it the way I see it, Sister Black. You got it like that, and you know I'm tellin' the truth."

"Well, I appreciate your observation, Miss Rayshonna," Mariah said. "But I will say this, it's not just about money and material possessions, it's about being happy. I always dreamed of having nice things, because I went without so many necessities when I was a child. But being happy and content is what's truly important."

Mariah wanted to make sure they understood that having a beautiful home, nice clothing, and a luxury vehicle didn't mean a thing if you weren't happy. She'd known that for years, but now she was learning it firsthand, in her marriage to Curtis. Although she hoped they were just going through a phase and that it would pass pretty quickly.

"I just hope I'll be able to go to college, too, once I get my GED," Ebony said. "I only have one more test to take next month, and then I'll have it."

"Good for you," Mariah said, and everyone applauded.

"Way to go, girlfriend," Rayshonna said, giving Ebony a high-five.

"I heard that," Shamira, a seventeen-year-old mother of two, said.

"We're going to celebrate big-time when you get it," Carmen insisted.

"That we will," Mariah guaranteed. "I'm not sure what we're going to do exactly, but we'll make sure it's something special."

"Now I can't wait until I get mine," Carmen said, smiling.

"You will," Mariah said. "You'll be finished with it before you know it."

Mariah's heart went out to all of the girls, but she had a very special place in it for Carmen. She was such a sweetheart and an amazing survivor. Her father had shot and killed her mother right in front of her when she was only five, and she'd lived with an aunt who physically abused her until she was twelve. Carmen had even shown everyone the print of an iron on her back, which was a result of her aunt chasing her. But eventually her aunt was reported by a neighbor and the authorities removed Carmen from the home. Then, as fate would have it, she was assigned to Sister Fletcher, a foster mother who was a member of the church. Sister Fletcher's husband was deceased and her biological children lived out of state, so she gave Carmen all the love and attention she needed. But when Carmen turned seventeen, she still dropped out of school. Sister Fletcher had told Mariah about it three months ago, and Mariah had suggested that Carmen attend the ministry meetings. Now she was doing a lot better emotionally and was attending an alternative school, working to complete her GED.

The girls spoke among themselves and Mariah noticed that it was almost time for them to end their session.

"I have something that I want all of you to read before our meeting next week," Mariah said, passing out booklets to each of them. "It's a book that specifically discusses how to find success in all areas of your life. It talks about the fact that you have to first believe in God, then believe in yourself, and then believe in whatever you're trying to accomplish. Because if your ability to believe manifests in that order, you'll quickly start to see positive changes in your life."

Everyone flipped curiously through the material and Mariah was glad they seemed interested.

"I think you'll enjoy reading this, and the other thing I want to keep encouraging all of you to do is stay prayerful. Prayer is very powerful when it comes from the heart, and I think you'll see God making a major difference in your life as you continue to communicate with Him. Prayer can give you so much peace, and regardless of what you are going through, God does hear all that you ask for."

"Then why doesn't He answer all the time?" Ebony wanted to know.

"Actually, He does, but it's just that He doesn't always answer when or in the way *we* want Him to. But He does always answer when the time is right. Sometimes we want what we want when we want it, but certain things aren't right for us. And then sometimes we want things to happen instantly, when it would be so much better if they happened at a later date. But that's just human nature, and it's perfectly normal to feel that way."

"I hear what you're saying, but it's still hard to understand sometimes," Ebony said.

"I know, but as you continue building your relationship with God, your understanding of Him and how He works will improve more and more."

"I agree," Carmen said matter-of-factly.

"Well, girls, unless you have something else you'd like to share this evening, I think it's time we dismissed."

Everyone agreed, the girls hugged Mariah and each other and then left the room.

Mariah couldn't help thinking about the advice she'd just given Ebony. Especially since she hadn't taken it herself when she met Curtis. She'd prayed over and over, asking God to make Curtis her husband, and it had happened. But now she wondered if God had actually blessed her with Curtis or simply allowed the marriage to happen because she wanted Curtis so badly. At the time, she hadn't cared about any possible consequences or even considered the fact that some people weren't nearly who they claimed to be, and she hoped she wasn't going to be sorry for it. She was such an optimist and had been told many times that she was much too trusting of people in general, but she couldn't help who she was. She'd always tried to do the right thing, and she always treated people the way she wanted to be treated. She couldn't understand why Curtis or anyone else would want to take advantage of that.

But maybe she was blowing her problems with Curtis way out of proportion. Maybe she was being too hard on him about all the time he was spending away from home, too. Because it wasn't like he had a normal nine-to-five. It wasn't like he could leave his work at the office when he was senior pastor of a church like Truth Missionary. The man had weekly sermons to write and preach, prayer service and Bible study to teach, the sick and shut-in to see, and sometimes he did revivals for out-of-town churches when they requested him. Of course, sometimes he received help from his associate ministers and deacons, but he really did have a whole lot of responsibilities. Maybe Curtis really was as busy as he claimed. Maybe she was expecting far too much from him and needed to find other things to do with her time, just as her mother had suggested. Her mother had also told her not to keep nagging Curtis, but that's exactly what she'd been doing. And it wasn't like he was staying out till the wee hours of the morning, anyway.

She decided that she wasn't giving up on him or their marriage. She was going to have faith in the love they shared and trust that everything would work out in the long run.

She decided it was best to stay positive and give her husband the total benefit of the doubt.

Chapter 9

Curtis drove through the intersection of Golf and Roselle over in Schaumburg. He was headed west toward Barrington and was on his way to visit some of his minister friends. He was also talking to Adrienne.

"You miss me?" he asked.

"You know I do," she said. "We've been together almost every other night, but I guess I just can't get enough of you. I haven't felt this good in a long time."

"Baby, neither have I, and if I hadn't promised the boys that I'd get together with them, I'd spend this evening with you, too. We only meet once a month, though, so I didn't want to renege on them."

"It's not a problem. But we are still on for Saturday, right?"

"Absolutely. Mariah is going shopping downtown with one of her girlfriends, so I'm all yours for the entire day."

"And you're sure your friend is okay with us using his condo?"

"Positive. I've already cleared it with him, and I'll be getting the key when I see him tonight."

"I can't believe it's in the same suburb where we used to rent ours."

"It's practically déjà vu."

"We were so happy back then."

"I know, baby, and I promise you we're going to be even happier this time around."

"That's what I keep hoping, Curtis, but I'm so afraid. I mean, I hear what you're saying, and I want to believe you, but I don't think I'll be completely comfortable with any of this until I see your divorce papers. And I think it's only fair for you to know that there is no way I can even consider leaving Thomas until then."

Curtis didn't like the sound of that. He didn't like it because more than anything, he wanted the deacon out of the picture. He needed him out of the way so that he could gain better control of Adrienne's emotions. He wasn't sure what he would have to do to convince her to get rid of the man, but he had to come up with something.

"I know I didn't do right by you before, but I'm telling you, baby, I'm totally committed to you for the rest of my life. Right now I'm in this situation with Mariah and you know it has to be handled very carefully, but I will divorce her."

"That's fine, but all I'm saying is that I won't leave Thomas until you show me proof in black and white."

"But don't you think it would look a lot better if you went ahead and divorced the deacon at least a few months before I divorce Mariah? Otherwise everyone will know we were planning this whole thing, and that we've been seeing each other all along."

"Maybe, but I can't do that. So as much as I love you, Curtis, and as much as I want to spend the rest of my life with you, these are the conditions."

"If that's how it has to be, then that's how it has to be."

"It does. And just so we're on the same page, we agreed last

Tuesday on the six-month time frame, so that means you have until the beginning of October to file for your divorce."

Curtis wanted to laugh out loud. He couldn't believe what he was hearing or that she was giving him an ultimatum so early in the relationship. She was acting as if they had a written contract, and Curtis could tell she was dead serious.

But he knew what he had to do. He had to keep seeing her three to four times a week like he used to. He'd make love to her in every way imaginable. So much so that she would no longer be able to think straight. She was trying very hard to stay in control, but when he finished with her on Saturday, she wouldn't know what hit her. She would beg to be with him under any circumstances.

But he decided to go along with what she was saying just to halt any confusion.

"The beginning of October it is. Or before if I can make it happen."

"I hate to be so technical about this, but it's the only way I can protect myself."

"I understand. But hey, I'm just pulling up to the condo, so I'd better go," he said, parking in the driveway behind a blue Jaguar and right next to a burgundy Escalade. There was also a black Lexus 430 parked closer to the garage.

"So I'll speak to you tomorrow?" she asked.

"I'll call you first thing in the morning when I get to the church. And don't you work too late."

"I'll try not to, but I'm working on this special marketing report that has to be finished by Monday morning. And it's not like I can come in on Saturday to do it."

"No, you definitely can't do it then, because you'll be with me until sundown."

"You know I'm looking forward to it. But I'll let you go, and you have a good time tonight."

"I love you, baby."

"I love you, too."

Curtis stepped out of the car, strolled up to the front door, and knocked.

"Hey, Rev, glad you could make it," Tyler said, opening the door of his four-bedroom condo. He was Curtis's closest minister friend and confidant.

"Me, too, man," Curtis said, hugging him.

Curtis shed his blazer, loosened his tie, and joined the three men at the glass table.

"You want anything to drink?" Tyler asked.

"Whatcha got?"

"Alize, Zinfandel, and I think there's some sort of Merlot in the fridge, too."

"Now, you Negroes know I don't drink intoxicating beverages," Curtis said.

"Oh yeah, that's right," Malcolm said, turning up a bottle of Miller Genuine Draft. "We forgot. You don't *drink*, you just sleep with as many women as you can."

They all roared with laughter.

"Well, I never said I was perfect, and y'all know from experience that some things are just too hard to give up," Curtis told them.

"I know that's right," Cletus said. "Because if I didn't have all those fine women at my church, I don't know what I would do. And that's the truth."

"God *is* good," Tyler added. "I mean, just look at this beautiful condo the church is paying for, and all I had to do was tell them I needed a retreat away from home. I told them that I needed somewhere I could go meditate, relax, and clear my head from time to time, and they totally went for it. They even agreed to purchase one this large because I told them we could also use it for out-of-town ministers and their families who were visiting our church. That way, they wouldn't have to stay at some hotel."

"Man, you got it made, because I would love to ask for something like this from Truth," Curtis said, admiring his surroundings. "But since I've only been there nine months, I figure I'd better take it slow when it comes to asking for more perks."

"You doin' the right thing, because you don't want them gettin' antsy about anything," Malcolm agreed. "If you ask for too much too fast, they'll start gettin' all suspicious on you."

"I second that motion," Cletus said. "Because the name of the game is trust. And once you have them trusting you one hundred percent, you can ask for practically anything you want. They'll be loving you and eating out of the palm of your hand without you even asking them to."

"And the women will do more than that," Tyler said. "They'll do any and everything you ask just because you're *the pastor*."

"I've got the four of mine so caught up that they all know about each other," Cletus said. "They pretend like they don't, but they all know exactly what's going on. And now I've gotten them so under control they're on a schedule."

"Man, you are too crazy," Malcolm said, cracking up.

"What kinda schedule?" Curtis asked, reaching inside a bowl of beer nuts.

"All four of them have a certain week of every month. I usually see them on Mondays, since that's my day off, and they each know which Monday is theirs."

"You have got to be kidding!" Tyler exclaimed, lifting a piece of pizza.

"I'm serious, man. Just like the mass choir sings on the first Sunday, the male chorus sings on the second, the young adults on the third, and the children on the fourth, I've got my women lined up the same way. If I didn't, how would I keep all of 'em straight?"

"You're a trip," Tyler said. "And if I were you I'd watch out before I ended up gettin' busted."

"No, see the difference between the three of y'all and me is that I stick with the young, dumb, and naïve ones," Cletus boasted. "That way, all you have to do is take 'em to a decent hotel and throw 'em a few dollars every now and then. After that, you have total control."

"You know, man, you might have something there," Curtis said. "Because now that I'm back with Adrienne—"

"What do you mean, now that you're back with Adrienne?" Tyler interrupted. "Last we heard, you'd seen her at some church concert but weren't planning to call her."

"Yeah," Malcolm teased. "You were going to be Mr. Nice and Faithful to your new wife, if I remember correctly."

"That's right," Cletus joked. "You were going to walk the straight and narrow until death do you part."

"Lord knows I tried, but it didn't work," Curtis admitted. "Anyway, we got together for dinner and then this past week I took her to a hotel a few times. But now she's ridin' me about divorcing Mariah."

"Already?" Tyler asked.

"Well, I sort of told her that I would do it in six months."

"You what?" Tyler exclaimed.

"Are you serious?" Cletus chimed in. "You really want to divorce that fine-ass Mariah?"

"No, I'm not divorcing anybody, but if I hadn't promised Adrienne that I would, she never would have started seeing me again. So I did what I had to do, but now she's issuing all these ultimatums."

"Man, you couldn't pay me to be in your shoes six months from now. That's for doggoned sure," Malcolm said.

"Me neither," Cletus said. "And I'd like to know exactly what you plan on doing about it."

"I don't know, but I'll think of something by then. Have to."

"You'd better," Tyler said. "Because somehow I don't think a woman like Adrienne will accept rejection all over again. I mean, you just don't keep playing with a woman who loves you the way Adrienne loved you before and obviously still loves you now."

"If I were you, I'd watch my back," Cletus said.

"Man, I don't think it's that serious," Curtis said confidently, but deep down he knew he had to craft something suitable before October. For the life of him he didn't know what excuse he could come up with, but he knew it had to be good. It had to be something that Adrienne would be pleased with.

"Alright, don't say we didn't try to warn you," Cletus said. "And it's because of mess like this that I don't deal with real women. They require way too much work, and it's so much easier when you stick with twenty-year-olds. As a matter of fact, once they turn twenty-five or so, I don't have much use for 'em."

"Well, as far as I'm concerned, I think you would all feel a whole lot safer if you stuck with one mistress," Tyler said. "I might dabble every now and then, but for the most part I stick with my wife and my main girl."

"I agree," Malcolm said. "One good mistress is more than adequate when you have a wife at home. And the only time I tend to stray is when I just can't help it. Because everyone here knows what it's like when certain out-of-town churches come to visit or you visit some out-of-town church and there's that certain woman who you just can't take your eyes off of."

"Yeah, I hear what you're saying, because even though I've dealt with multiple women in the past, I'm going to try to stick with just one from now on," Curtis said. "And I've definitely learned my lesson about dealing with women inside my own church. So that's totally off-limits."

"Well, I'm sticking with my four," Cletus argued.

"We don't doubt that," Tyler teased. "But hey, on a different note, Curtis, man, did you talk to your officers about installing those ATM machines and offering direct deposit to your members?"

"Man, yeah. But they weren't too receptive. And two of the older deacons practically lost it. They acted like I was planning to commit a felony or somethin'."

"I'm sorry to hear that, because when I spoke with mine, they wanted to know more. They also didn't see a problem with us hiring financial planners," Tyler said.

"But, see, that's the thing with your officers, they hired you to lead the church, and they're allowing you to do it," Curtis acknowledged. "And even though I have a lot of young officers and a few from the old church, they're too afraid to stand up for what they believe in. Some of them are a little on the conservative side, too."

"Then what you have to do is find some skeletons," Cletus said.

"Meaning what?"

"Meaning you need to talk to some of those gossip columnists at your church. Every congregation has 'em, and I'm sure they'll be more than happy to tell you what they know about your little deacon board. Because you can bet your last dollar that every one of 'em has something in his past or something he's doing right now that would give you grounds to make him step down from the board. And push come to shove, I would hire a private investigator if I had to."

"I really hadn't considered anything like that, but you might have a point," Curtis agreed, and wished he'd thought of that himself. If he could get rid of Deacon Thurgood and Deacon Winslow, he'd be halfway to the finish line.

"You've got to do what you have to do when you're dealing with some of these fools. Otherwise you'll be fighting a losing battle for all eternity," Cletus said matter-of-factly.

"Yeah, you do have to get rid of the ones who won't go along with the program," Malcolm said. "I did that five years ago, and I haven't had any problems ever since."

"It's a shame, but they're right, Curtis," Tyler said. "You have to get a group of men who will let you do what you think is best when it comes to running *your* church. You need to make sure that at least ninety-five percent of your officers are pro-Curtis Black before you try to approach them with that ATM and direct deposit proposal again. But you do need to take care of it at some point, because if you can get the direct deposit thing going, Cletus and Malcolm can show you how to funnel some of it into your own account."

"And in the future, you need to make sure that every deacon and trustee you appoint is a very able lieutenant. You have to make sure they have the balls to back you up in front of anybody," Cletus said.

Curtis nodded. "I should have done that when I was at Faith, because if I had, I might still be pastor over there."

"You probably would be," Tyler said. "Because it sounds like your main rival was Deacon Jackson, and it's not that hard to get rid of one man."

Curtis was glad he had three true friends in his age range who were successful senior pastors. Each of them was the man he wanted to be when he grew up. They were the men he was on his way to being before he was kicked out of the pulpit. Curtis had always taken great pride in knowing that he was on top of things and that he had a good head on his shoulders, but Tyler, Malcolm, and Cletus were on a different level. They'd all been in their positions for eight or more years and each had his entire church under command. They also had a ton more members than Curtis. Tyler, Curtis's knight in shining armor, had over ten thousand members. Malcolm had around eight, and Cletus had just over six. They were the true definition of success, and Curtis had learned a long time ago that if a person truly wanted to be successful they needed to network with those who were doing much better than them. They needed to watch and learn from people who were already what and where they aspired to be.

"So which flick are we going to indulge tonight?" Cletus asked, walking over to Tyler's brand-spanking-new forty-two-inch plasma TV.

"Man, I hadn't even noticed your new screen," Curtis said, turning around. "How much did that set you back?"

"It set *New Hope* back about seven grand, and the thing is, I didn't even ask for it," Tyler said. "One of my trustees is manager at some electronics store, and he suggested to the entire board that it would be nice for me to have the latest technology. So after discussing it, they decided it would make the perfect birthday gift from the church."

"That's how it's supposed to be," Cletus said. "Every church should take care of its pastor before it does anything else."

"I do have to admit, they *are* very generous to my family and me," Tyler said. "Tina thinks the world of just about everyone at the church, and my two daughters feel the same way."

"I can see why," Curtis said. "My congregation feels the same way about Mariah and me, too, and it does give you a good feeling."

"So which one will it be, boys?" Cletus reiterated, flipping through a stack of DVDs. "Or maybe we should order pay-per-view through the satellite."

"Man, you must be crazy," Tyler said. "You know the title of the movie will show up on the bill and the bill goes straight to the church."

"Oh, that's right. My bad, brother."

"Wouldn't that be somethin'," Malcolm said, laughing.

"So I think you'd better pick one of those in that stack," Tyler said.

Cletus flipped through them again and said, "*Beautiful Black Bunnies* it is."

Chapter 10

"Mom, do you think James will take me to the father-daughter dance in a couple of weeks?" Alicia asked, leaning against the island. At first she'd decided not to go, but after Danielle practically begged her to change her mind, she did. And she had another motive, too.

"I'm sure he would be honored, but are you sure you don't want to ask your father?" Tanya said, tossing a bowl of lettuce. They were just preparing to sit down for dinner as soon as James came back downstairs.

"No, because, like always, he's probably too busy."

Alicia didn't want her father to escort her anyway, and she was going to make sure to brag to him about her night out with James just so it would piss him off. She wanted him to know, for a change, what it felt like to be disappointed.

"You won't know unless you ask him," Tanya said.

"But, Mom, I don't want Daddy to take me. And if that's who has to do it, I won't go at all. James is the one who spends time with me and who takes my friends and me anywhere we want to go. He even takes us with him to see the Bears and the Bulls when they play at home."

"I understand that, Alicia, and I'm glad you appreciate James as much as you do, but I still don't want you to overlook your father. I know he's made some mistakes, but this might be a good opportunity for you to spend some time with him alone. Especially since that's what you've been saying you want."

"I did, but now I'm through with him. I don't care if I ever see him again, and even when I get married one day, I'm having James walk me down the aisle," Alicia said, and felt like bawling. She hated her father for neglecting her the way he was, and she was going to make him pay for it. She didn't want to use James to punish her father, because she did genuinely love James, but she just didn't know what else to do to get her father's attention.

"I think you should talk to James about it to see what he thinks."

Alicia took the salad bowl and sat it on the table near the patio doors. Then she brought over a pan filled with warm garlic bread. Her mother had fixed her famous lasagna and Alicia couldn't wait to eat some of it.

"By the way, I called your counselor today, and he said you haven't missed one class this week, and that you've turned in all of your history assignments," Tanya said. "So that's why, even though you're still grounded, I'm okay with you going to the dance."

Alicia didn't know what to say. She was a little perturbed that her mother saw a need to keep checking up on her, but she wasn't going to make a big deal out of it. Maybe last week she would have, but not after chatting with Julian on-line a couple of days ago. He'd told her that life would be a lot easier if she simply went to class and did her homework. That way, her parents wouldn't have anything to complain about, and they wouldn't have a reason to keep punishing her. She hadn't agreed at first, but there were two things he'd said that had made her rethink her position. He'd told her that even though she was angry, she needed to remember everything her mother had gone through with her father and be thankful that James was the sort of stepfather that treated her like his own. He told her that, to him, it seemed like her mother and James were always there for her and that she should work very hard at trying to appreciate that.

She still didn't like the fact that her mother was trying to control her life, but she had to agree with what Julian said. Her mother *had* been a good wife to her father, and she'd always gone out of her way to be a good mother. When she was married to her father and even now that she was married to James. So Alicia decided she was going to do the right thing when it came to school, but she wasn't going to let her father off so easily.

"Boy, that smells even better than before I went upstairs," James said, playfully yanking Alicia's ponytail as he walked by her.

"Stop it," Alicia said, laughing.

Tanya smiled at both of them and sat down at the table. Alicia and James did the same.

"Do you want to say grace, Alicia?" Tanya asked.

They all held hands and closed their eyes. "Dear Lord, thank You for my mom, thank You for James, and thank You for the food we're about to receive. Amen."

Tanya and James spoke in unison. "Amen."

"This is still sort of hot," Tanya said, scooping out a square of lasagna and placing it on James's plate. Then she put a piece on Alicia's and then hers.

"So how was school today?" James said, picking up the tongs inside the salad bowl.

"Didn't Mom tell you?"

"Tell me what?"

"That I haven't missed any more classes, and I've turned in all of my history homework."

"No, she didn't, but I'm really glad to hear that, because I was starting to worry about you."

"I think we were all worried," Tanya said.

Alicia knew her mother was including her father when she said "all," but Alicia knew he didn't care one way or the other. The only thing he cared about were his precious little Mariah, that new church of his, and how much more money he could get.

"I still scheduled a counseling session for us next week, though," Tanya said.

"Not with Daddy, too, I hope."

"Yes, with Daddy, too."

Alicia pursed her lips.

"It's for you, him, and me," Tanya continued. "And in the future, we can include James and Mariah if you want."

Mariah? For what? She wasn't Alicia's mother, and she was never going to get a chance to be. So why would she possibly need to come to counseling with them? If Alicia had anything to say about it, it would never happen. Mariah was an outsider, and it was best for her to stay where she belonged: outside.

But Alicia wasn't going to share her thoughts out loud.

"James, can you take me to the father-daughter dance in a couple of weeks?"

"Well, pumpkin, you know I'd be happy to, but I don't want to disrespect your father either."

"You won't, because I'm sure he already has other plans."

"Have you asked him?"

"No. He always has other plans."

"But I still think you should ask him. You know? Just out of respect."

"Why? Don't you want to take me?"

"Yes. You know I do, but it's just that I think you should at least acknowledge your father."

"But I don't want him to take me."

"I think you do, and you're only saying that because you want to hurt him."

Alicia didn't know how he knew what she was thinking, but he had her pegged to a tee.

Tanya looked on in silence.

"Look, Alicia," James said, tearing a piece of garlic bread. "I know you haven't been too happy with your father lately, but I think you need to give him another chance. I'm not trying to make excuses for him, but we all make mistakes from time to time."

"Daddy makes mistakes *all* the time, and ever since he married Mariah, he hasn't cared one thing about me." Alicia swallowed hard, trying to stop tears from rolling down her face.

"That's not true, Alicia," Tanya said. "Your father may have a strange way of showing it, but he does love you. It's the one thing I can say about him."

"Then why doesn't he act like it?" Alicia said, wiping her face, her chest elevating.

"We can't answer that, sweetheart, but don't ever think that he doesn't love you," Tanya said, holding Alicia's hand. "Because he truly, truly does."

"So why don't you give him a call when we finish dinner," James said. "If he says he can't take you, then two Saturdays from now, it'll be you and me out on the town. But I at least want you to ask him."

None of this had turned out the way Alicia had wanted. She'd planned on having James escort her, and then she was planning to parade tons of photos of them in front of her father. She wanted him to know how it felt to be left out and replaced. But now James and her mother had made her realize that she did want her father to take her. He probably already had some previous church engagement, but she would call him like James suggested.

They continued eating and discussed the fact that Easter was this weekend, that there were only six more weeks of school, and that they were taking a family vacation to Disney World at the end of June. Alicia was even more excited when they told her Danielle could go with them to Orlando.

After Alicia finished loading the dishes in the dishwasher, she went up to her room to call her father.

"Hello," Mariah answered.

Alicia rolled her eyes toward the ceiling.

"Hi, Mariah. Is my daddy there?"

"No, honey, he's not. He got together with some other ministers for a meeting, but you can call him on his cell phone if you need him right away."

"Okay, then, thanks."

"Alicia?" Mariah said.

"Yes."

"Can I talk to you for a minute?"

About what? was all Alicia could think to say.

"What did you wanna talk about?"

"Well, basically I just wanted to tell you that I'm here for you if you ever need me, and that I'm hoping you can start spending more time over here with your father and me."

What Alicia wanted was to spend more time with her father. Not with Mariah.

"Okay," Alicia said just to hurry her off the phone.

"And while I know I haven't been your stepmother for very long, I'm really hoping that we can start building a relationship with each other. Maybe we could go shopping together. Summer will be here pretty soon, so maybe we could get you a whole new summer wardrobe."

"Actually, my mom is taking me shopping for summer stuff next week."

"Well, I know it's a little late, but have you already gotten an Easter outfit?"

Duh. Easter was only three days from now, so what did she think?

"My mom bought my Easter dress sometime last month, but thanks for asking."

"Well, maybe we can do something else. I remember you saying that you weren't coming to stay with us this weekend since it's Easter, so can we expect you next weekend?"

"Actually, I have a father-daughter dance to go to, and I want my mom to help me get ready for it," Alicia bragged, but felt like kicking herself because she hadn't wanted Mariah to know about the dance until after she'd told her father.

"Oh, is that why you're calling your father? He'll be so excited. I never got to do things like that with my father when I was growing up, because he never came around."

Then, that means you know exactly how I feel, don't you? Alicia thought.

"Well, it was good talking to you, Mariah, but I'd better go so I can call my daddy."

"It was good talking to you, Alicia, and remember what I said, you can call me anytime."

"Okay, bye."

Alicia pressed the flash button and dialed her father's cell number.

"Hi, baby girl," he answered.

"How'd you know it was me?"

"Caller ID of course."

"Oh."

"So how are you?"

"I'm fine, but who's making all that noise in the background?"

"Those are just some other ministers having a few laughs. But hold on a minute while I go into another room."

They sounded like wild animals instead of ministers, but she wasn't going to tell her father what she was thinking.

"Okay, so to what do I owe this precious phone call?" he said.

"My school is having a ninth-grade father-daughter dance on the twenty-sixth, and I wanted to see if you could take me."

"Of course I can, baby girl. You know I wouldn't have it any other way. What time is it?"

"Six o'clock, and you have to wear a tux."

"Well, you know I already have one of those, so I'm all set. But what about you? Do you already have a dress for it?"

"No, but I'm sure Mom will take me out this weekend to get one."

"Well, if she can't, you know Mariah would be happy to take you, too."

"No, that's okay, I'll just have Mom do it."

"Well, I'm glad you called me, baby girl, because I haven't heard from you since you spent the weekend with us. I'm sorry for yelling at you, but the last thing I want to see is you failing one of your classes. You're too smart for that, and I won't be content until you've graduated from high school and gone on to college. I've been saving for your college education since the day you were born, and even though I had a setback when I left Faith, I never took any money from that account. So you getting the right education is very, very important to me."

Alicia was a little shocked at what she was hearing. She'd heard him mention a college fund when she was younger, but she hadn't heard him talk much about it in the last few years. At least he cared about something that had to do with her, and while she still wasn't happy with him, she was elated to know that he was saving money for her education. Most of her friends couldn't care less about their parents saving for college, but Alicia knew just how expensive it actually was.

"I know it is, Daddy, and that's why I've turned in all of my history assignments." She wasn't sure if he knew about her skipping an entire week of math classes or not, so there was no sense in bringing it up.

"I'm glad to hear it. So tell me, how's your mom doing?"

"She's fine."

"Tell her I said hello, and that if she needs money to get your dress, she can call me."

"I will."

"And, Alicia?"

"Yes."

"You do know that I love you, right?"

"Yes."

"I know I haven't always done the right things, but next to God, you really are the most important person in my life."

"Then why don't we spend time together the way we used to before you married Mariah?" she asked, though she hadn't meant to.

"Is that what you think? That Mariah is the reason I haven't been able to see you as much?"

"Yes, because we did a lot of stuff together before you met her."

"Well, let Daddy tell you a little secret. Mariah complains almost every day because she says I'm not spending any time with her either. So, baby girl, it has absolutely nothing to do with her and everything to do with the fact that I'm trying to get situated at my new church. I have the same responsibilities that I had when I was pastor at Faith and a whole new set of duties to go along with them."

"Well, I still wish you'd make more time for me, because I miss seeing you," Alicia said, and wondered if her father was telling the truth. If he was, she was glad to know that he hadn't placed Mariah higher than her on his list of priorities.

"I miss you too, and I'm going to try to do better, starting with your dance next week."

"Okay, well, I'd better let you go, Daddy. But don't forget, it's at six o'clock on Saturday. Not this Saturday, but the next one."

"I won't forget. I'll have Whitney put it on my schedule, and I'll also put it in my Palm Pilot. And, baby girl, you know you should come hear your daddy preach this Sunday for Easter."

"I already told Mom and James that I was going with them to our church," she said, knowing full well her mother and stepfather wouldn't have minded one way or the other.

"Oh well, I just thought I'd ask. Maybe another time then. Also, I guess I'll see you next week, because your mom left me a voice message a few days ago saying we have a counseling session scheduled."

"Yeah, we do."

"Okay, well, I'll see you then, baby girl."

"Okay. Good-bye, Daddy."

"I love you."

"I love you, too."

Alicia hung up the phone feeling happier than she had in a long time. She couldn't wait to tell Julian how good his advice had been and how she was finally working things out with her parents. She was still sorry that she'd laughed at him that day he'd tried to have phone sex with her, but now at least he wasn't angry anymore. He wasn't angry because she'd called him back the very next night and two other nights thereafter and did everything he told her to do. She'd experienced sensations she didn't even know existed, and she wished she could feel that good all the time.